THE LAIRD'S BRIDE

**A Stand-Alone
Scottish Novella**

ANNE GRACIE

Praise for
Anne Gracie's Books:

"You can't do much better than Anne Gracie who offers her share of daring escapes, stolen kisses, and heartfelt romance in a tale that carries the effervescent charm of the best Disney fairy-tales." — *Entertainment Weekly*

For Marry In Haste:

VERDICT: With deep character insight, subtle humor matched with rapier wit, and brilliant repartee, Gracie puts a refreshing spin on a classic romance trope and delivers another knockout Regency that will keep fans enthralled. — *Library Journal* (starred review)

For The Autumn Bride:

"Gracie charms and entices with this launch of the Regency-era Chance Sisters series . . . Layers of secrets and deft characterization make for a deep, rich story that will leave readers starry-eyed."—*Publishers Weekly* (starred review)

"The Chance sisters are living a dream, and readers will be thrilled to be there with them. Gracie has created a wonderful cast of characters, from the sisters themselves to their benefactress and servants . . . The lively dialogue and tender emotions compel readers to relish every moment."—RT Book Reviews (Top Pick)

"I honestly can't remember the last time I've enjoyed a book quite this much . . . I predict *The Autumn Bride* is going to be *the* book to add to the TBR list of historical romance fans everywhere."—Night Owl Reviews

For To Catch a Bride:

VERDICT: "Threaded with charm and humor, this action-rich, emotionally compelling story is the third in Gracie's popular "Devil Riders" series. Though it stands on its own, it is sure to entice readers to read the others." — Library Journal

"There is so much I liked about this one, it's hard to find a place to start... Anne Gracie's TO CATCH A BRIDE kept me flipping pages in a rush to get to the ending, only to want just a little more." — All About Romance

"I'm happy to report that TO CATCH A BRIDE is a Keeper." — Rakehell

""A fascinating twist on the girl-in-disguise plot, Anne Gracie's To Catch A Bride pits a raffish aristocrat aganst a tough little street boy — but he's no boy... With its wildly romantic last chapter, this novel is a great antidote to the end of the summer." — Eloisa James, author

For The Winter Bride:

VERDICT: "A pretend engagement devolves into a forced marriage when plans go awry in this exquisitely written, perfectly plotted story that features deeply wounded but resilient protagonists and introduces an intriguing, most unconventional new character." — *Library Journal* (starred review)

For The Christmas Bride:

"The many readers already familiar with Anne Gracie's Chance Sisters novels will love *The Christmas Bride*. . . snip . . . Lovely and heartwarming, it will provide a blissful escape for an afternoon curled up by a fire, a cup of hot chocolate at the ready." — *AustenProse*

DEAR READER,

A couple of years ago, in response to many lovely reader emails, I decided to write and self-publish a novella about Blake Ashton, *The Chance Sisters* series. That story became *The Christmas Bride* and its success was very encouraging. Thank you so much to everyone who bought it, read it and left a rating or review. I'm very grateful.

The Laird's Bride was originally a short story called The Laird's Vow, commissioned back in 2010 at a maximum length of 12,000 words for the Mammoth Book of Scottish Romance (now out of print). Readers said they enjoyed my story, but that it was too short and the end was rushed — and they were right.

But I liked the story and wanted to show my hero and heroine—who married as strangers—really falling in love, so I decided to go back and write it at the length it needed to be, and publish it myself. It's now three times the length it was. If you read the original short story, the first third of the novella will be very familiar, but from the wedding night onwards, it's all new.

Those of you who've read my other books will know that this is my first and only Scottish romance. But I've been in love with Scotland most of my life, since the age of seven, when my family moved to Scotland for my dad's job. As "the wee Australian girl" whose schoolfellows fell silent every time I opened my mouth, I soon developed a broad Scots accent, and while I was writing this story, the cadence and accents of my childhood returned to mind and made their way into this book. As well, my father's side of the family is also Scottish, and before I ever set foot on Scottish soil, I had learned to say The Selkirk Grace, by Robbie Burns, at mealtimes. When I went to school in Scotland, of course, my accent improved, and I learned a lot more of his poems and songs, including the one quoted at the end.

I hope you enjoy *The Laird's Bride*.

Anne

Chapter One

"**Y**OU'RE LETTING THE estate run to rack and ruin!" Cameron Fraser thundered.

"Nonsense, dear boy, I'm bringing civilization to it," his uncle responded. "Thirty years I've lived here" — he shuddered — "and finally it's within my power to make something of the place."

"Make something of it? You're letting it fall to pieces. The great storm was more than two months ago and not one tenant's roof is yet repaired, nor any orders given to begin. Winter's staring us in the face, and what do you do, Uncle? Order silk hangings from Paris—silk!"

His uncle said earnestly, "But dear boy, quality pays. Wait 'til you see what a difference hangings will make to this gloomy room. Besides, the tenants can fix their own roofs."

Cameron's nails bit into his palms. "Not without money to pay for materials, they can't. Besides, it's our responsibility — my responsibility as laird."

His uncle smiled. "Laird? In name, perhaps."

"Aye, I ken well it's in name only. Yet I bear all the shame for the neglect," Cameron said bitterly. "If Uncle Ian were still alive . . ."

"I know. Who would have imagined he'd go before me, him being so much younger, but there it is," Charles Sinclair said. "So you'll just have to trust me. I have so many plans. Nearly five years is it not, before you turn thirty and gain control?"

Cameron clenched his jaw. After his father had died, both of Cameron's uncles had been left in charge, and he'd paid scant attention to estate finances. Uncle Ian was a Fraser, and his love for the estate and its people ran bone deep in him, as it did in Cameron. But now Uncle Ian was dead and the remaining trustee, his maternal uncle, Charles Sinclair, could do as he pleased. And what he pleased was, in Cameron's view, entirely frivolous.

Cameron tried again. "If those roofs aren't fixed, come winter, people will freeze. Do you want the death of women and bairns on your conscience?"

Charles Sinclair returned to the perusal of silk swatches. "Your conscience is too delicate, dear boy. Peasants are hardy folk. Now, look at this design I drew for—"

"You'll not spend a shilling more of my inheritance!"

His uncle glanced up, faintly amused. "Dear boy, how do you propose stopping me?"

"Marriage!" The word burst from Cameron's mouth, shocking himself as well as his uncle. He'd had no intention of marrying, not for years to come, but now he saw it was his only solution. Under the rules of his father's will the trust would conclude on Cameron's thirtieth birthday or his wedding day—whichever came first.

"Marriage? With whom, pray? You've not attended a society event in years."

It was true. Cameron preferred hunting and

fishing to dancing and, up to now, he'd avoided the marriage mart of Inverness like the plague. As a result he couldn't think of a single likely female. And since half the women on the estate were related to him, officially or unofficially—Grandad had been quite a lusty lad—he had to look further afield.

Cameron's fists clenched in frustration.

His uncle chuckled. "You haven't thought it through, dear boy, have you? Marriages take time to arrange. Your grandfather and mine negotiated for months over my dear sister's marriage to your father, and as your trustee, naturally I will handle any such negotiations on your behalf. And by then you will have a home worthy of a bride." He patted his designs.

"No negotiations will be necessary," Cameron snapped. "I'll marry the first eligible woman I find." He turned on his heel and stormed from the room, nearly cannoning into his two cousins, Jimmy and Donald, waiting outside. Distant cousins, orphaned and raised on the estate, they were like brothers to Cameron.

"What did he—" Donald began.

"Meet you at the stables in fifteen minutes," Cameron snapped. "I'm off to Inverness to find a bride."

———

The three young men galloped through the village, scattering squawking hens and setting dogs barking. "Marry the first eligible woman you find? You canna be serious!" Donald shouted over the sound of galloping hooves.

"Ye're crazy, mon," Jimmy agreed. "If ye must marry, at least choose the lass wi' care and caution."

"I've no choice," Cameron flung back. "The longer I leave it the more my uncle squanders what little money we have. He's already ordered silk hangings from Paris—costing a fortune. The sooner I'm wed, the sooner I can cancel the order. And stop his ridiculous spending."

Rain set in, a thin, relentless drizzle. After half an hour of it Jimmy edged his horse alongside Cameron. "Ach, Cameron this rain is freezin' me to death. Let's go back. We'll find a solution to your woes tomorrow, when we're no' such sodden miseries."

"You go back if you want to, I'm for Inverness. I swore I'd marry the first eligible woman I find, and so I will." Cameron bent his head against the rain and rode on.

"He swore to his uncle he'd marry," Jimmy told his brother glumly. He pulled out a flask, took a swig of whisky and passed it across.

Donald drank from it. "He'll no go back on his word then. You know Cameron."

"Aye, pigheaded—a Fraser to the bone." Jimmy drank another dram of whisky and the two brothers rode gloomily on in their cousin's wake.

Cameron took no notice. He was used to his cousin's complaints. They'd stick with him, he knew. He was glad of it. Another few hours to Inverness, and then to find a bride. The whole idea was somewhat . . . daunting.

He'd never given marriage much thought. He liked women well enough, but mariage was a serious business, the sort of thing a man considered in his thirties. But he couldn't let his uncle squander any more of his inheritanc

Cameron's mother and her brother, though of pure Scots blood, had been born and raised in France. Their grandparents were exiles who'd fled with the Prince after the disaster of Culloden. Raised in Parisian luxury, fed on romantic, impossible dreams of Scottish glory, they'd both found Scottish reality, and the poverty that had resulted from the effects of war, sorely disappointing.

Cameron's mother had died of an ague when he was a wee lad, but her brother, Charles, who'd initially come for the wedding, had stayed on, never marrying, seemingly harmless. Cameron's father had tolerated him, and Cameron was inclined to do the same. Blood was blood, after all.

Though to name him as co-trustee . . .

Who would have expected Uncle Ian Fraser to sicken and die of a chill, such a big, hale man he'd been?

But if, after nearly thirty years of sponging off the Frasers, Charles Sinclair thought he could now turn a Scottish castle into a mini Versailles, he had another think coming.

They reached the bog at the southern edge of the estate. A narrow raised road had been built across it in ages past. At the end of the causeway was the wooden bridge that would take him onto the Inverness road.

In ancient times the bog had proved a useful barrier. The estate lay on a promontory, defended on two sides by water, and inland by mountains. The narrow, easily defended causeway was the only way to cross the treacherous, muddy land of the promontory, and the bridge over the burn into which the bog slowly drained gave the only access to it. History had lost count of the number of times Frasers had burned the bridge to keep out invaders.

But those times were long past. The current bridge had been built when his grandfather was a boy. It was time to drain the bog and build a sturdy stone bridge, Cameron thought. His father had planned to do it but he'd died.

God grant Cameron would soon have the power to begin the necessary work. All he needed was a wife. It wouldn't take him long, surely, in a town the size of Inverness.

Chapter Two

HIS SPIRITS LIFTING, Cameron urged his horse along the causeway, galloping into the rain.

A herd of sheep suddenly appeared, ghostly in the misty drizzle, bunched thick along the causeway, blocking the road. Cameron hauled his horse to a standstill. It snorted and moved restlessly, misliking the situation.

The sheep eyed Cameron suspiciously and backed away, but, "Get on there!" a voice shouted from behind the herd. "You on the horses, stand still and let the sheep through!"

Cameron squinted into the rain. Dimly he could see a boy in a too-big coat and hat, waving a crook. A dog barked and the sheep bunched and milled and baaaed uncertainly, crowding to the very edge of the causeway.

Behind him Jimmy and Donald's horses plunged to a halt. "Get those beasties out of the way," Jimmy shouted.

"Dinna shout at them, ye fool," the boy snapped. "They're foolish beasts and are like to panic. And if any get into the bog . . ."

Jimmy, being well into the contents of his flask, was inclined to argue—gentlemen on horseback took precedence over sheep—but Cameron held up his hand. "Stay still," he ordered.

The dog barked again and suddenly the first sheep darted past Cameron. The milling herd followed, streaming around and past the men on horseback like a living river, baaing madly, their long sodden woolen skirts swinging as they fled along the causeway. Two little black-faced lambs, however, plunged off the causeway and floundered in the muddy bog. Their mother followed.

"Och, ye fool beasties!" The boy followed them into the bog with a splash. He grabbed the first lamb and set it back on its feet. It stood, bleating plaintively. The boy then began to heave at the mother, both of them floundering in the mud. Jimmy and Donald grinning, watched the show from horseback.

Cameron barely noticed. The rain had eased and he could see the bridge, a few dozen yards away. Or what remained of the bridge. It was impassable, smashed to pieces, looking more like the scattering of a giant's matchsticks than a bridge.

It must have happened during the great storm. Rage slowly filled him. His uncle must have known. And he'd done nothing. This was as bad, or worse than the roofs needing repairs. The bridge gave the estate direct access to the Inverness road.

Uncle Charles, however, only cared about access to France, and that was by boat, not road.

Cameron stared at the devastation. He'd have to return the way he'd come, and leave by the westerly border. It would take hours longer.

"Give it up, Cam." His cousin Donald touched his arm. "We've no choice but to turn back now. It'll be dark before we even get home."

"I'll no' go home wi' my tail between my legs," Cameron muttered, though in truth he could see no other alternative. "And I'll not leave the estate in my uncle's hands a day longer than I must."

"There's naught you can do wi' the bridge in that state, though, is there?" Donald said reasonably. "Ye canna cross it; ye must go back."

"Dammit, I can see that!" Thwarted and furious, Cameron glared at the bridge. Hearing laughter behind him, he turned to see his cousin Jimmy swigging whisky and chuckling at the spectacle of the boy still trying to rescue the wretched ewe. The large, ungainly animal was plunging deeper into the bog, struggling desperately, as if the lad were trying to drown it instead of saving it. From where Cameron stood, the sheep was winning. Both lad and beast were black mud to the eyebrows. And on the far side of the struggle the remaining small lamb was sinking fast.

"Make yourself useful, will ye Jimmy? Give the lad a hand."

Jimmy snorted. "And get my new boots filled with black mud?"

Cameron glanced at Donald, who shrugged and made no move. The lad fell for the third time. The tiny lamb struggled to keep its head above the muddy water.

Cameron swore, swung off his horse and waded in. He scooped the lamb out first and set it on its feet beside its twin. Then he hauled the boy out, shoving him close to the bank. "Jimmy! Pull him out."

Jimmy dismounted, gingerly took the boy's dirty hands and dragged him onto the solid causeway. Cameron waded back in and tried to fetch the mother sheep. The stupid thing bucked and fought, and in seconds Cameron himself was black with bog mud.

His cousins watched from the bank, passing the flask back and forth, making bets and roaring with laughter.

But Cameron was strong and big and angry. He wrapped his arms around the sheep's middle and heaved the filthy beast onto the bank, causing his cousins to leap back like fine ladies to avoid the mud. The sheep shook itself, bleated and trotted indignantly away, followed by the lambs.

Cameron's cousins were laughing fit to burst. He'd fix them. "Help me out." He held out his hands, but they laughed and backed away.

"We're no so far gone we'd fall for that old trick," Jimmy chortled.

"Canny bastards," Cameron muttered as he climbed out of the bog, black mud dripping from him. "And if there's no whisky left in that flask, I swear I'll throw you in anyway."

Laughing, Jimmy tossed him the flask. Cameron was about to drain it when he saw how the shepherd lad was shivering in the cold. He thrust it toward the boy, saying, "Here, lad, you need this more than me."

The boy accepted it with a surprised expression and took a quick swig. He shuddered violently as the whisky went down, but managed to gasp out his thanks.

"So, boy," Cameron said. "What's your name?"

The shepherd boy gave a quick grin, a cheeky white slash in a muddy face. "Jeannie McLeay, sir, and thank you for getting the sheep out o' the mud, even if you and your friends did panic the beasts in the first place. My grandad would've kilt me if I'd lost her." She tried to wipe the mud off her face with her sleeve and only smeared it more.

"Jeannie?" Cameron stared. The coat she wore was a man's coat, too big for her, rolled up at the sleeves and hanging down almost to her ankles, but though it was hard to tell because of the mud, there was a skirt beneath it. The boots she wore were a man's boots, too big, surely for her feet and the hat crammed on her head was a man's hat.

"Are ye married, Jeannie?" Jimmy asked, suddenly intent.

She frowned. "No," she said cautiously.

"And where were ye born?"

"Stop that!" Cameron snapped, realizing what his cousin was up to.

Jimmy gave him an innocent look. "No harm in asking."

"Drop it, Jimmy," Cameron told his cousin. He was not going to marry some ragamuffin he'd dragged out of a bog.

"She's the first one you've seen," Jimmy insisted.

"The first what?" the girl demanded.

"He couldna take her anyway," Donald argued. "She's just a wee thing, no' a grown woman."

"Take me where? Nobody's taking me anywhere."

"Stow it you two, the whole idea's ridiculous," Cameron said. His cousins took no notice. There was a bet on and the contents of the flask were obviously well absorbed.

"How old are you, Jeannie lass?" Jimmy asked.

"Nineteen," Jeannie McLeay said, eying each man suspiciously. "But as I said, nobody's taking me anywhere." She began to edge away.

Jimmy grabbed her by the arm, careless now of

any mud, intent only on his wager. "And where were you born, Jeannie, me dear?"

"I'm no' your dear." She yanked her arm from his grip and hurried away, flinging over her shoulder, "And not that it's any of your business, but I was born on the isle of Lewis."

At her words, Jimmy let out a whoop of triumph and punched his brother in the shoulder. "Lewis! She's eligible! You owe me a monkey, Donald!"

"The bet's no' won 'til the deed is done," Donald insisted. "Cameron's yet to wed her."

"He will, he will," Jimmy crowed.

Donald snorted. "It's a crazy notion, and Cameron's no' the crazy one here."

Jimmy shook his head. "He gave his word, man, and Cameron never goes back on his word."

The girl followed her sheep, putting as much distance between herself and the men as she could, running swiftly despite the clumsy, man-sized boots. Cameron watched her thoughtfully.

When he'd made his rash statement he had no thought of wedding anyone except a lady born. This bog sprite shepherdess was totally unsuitable.

But he'd never broken his word before. Rashness gave way to serious thought; there might be wives to be had in Inverness—ladies—but how long would it take to get one to wed him? And how much would his uncle squander in the meantime?

Jimmy grabbed him by the shoulder. "Well, Cammie, will ye wed her or no? There's a bet on."

Cameron swore softly under his breath. The girl was young, unmarried and born outside the estate. What difference would it make anyway who he wed? Women were for running the house and birthing babes and any female could do that, surely. Getting control of his inheritance was what counted. Besides, the little he knew of ladies born was that they were a lot of trouble. They expected a man to dance attendance on them, whereas a lass like this, country bred and down-to-earth . . . He looked at her retreating form. Mud dripped off her with every step. Very down-to-earth.

"Aye, I'll wed her," he declared.

"Aha—" Jimmy began, then let out a yell. "She's getting away. Don't worry, Cam, I'll get her back for ye." And without warning he jumped on his horse and galloped after the girl.

"Och, the mad fool," Donald said. "Whatever will the lassie think—"

Cameron leapt on his horse and set off after Jimmy.

The girl, seeing Jimmy bearing down on her, screamed defiance at him and ran faster. Jimmy let out a whoop, as if he was running down a hind.

"Leave her be, Jimmy," Cameron roared.

But Jimmy was almost on the girl and oblivious. With a blood-curdling yell he scooped her up and tossed her over his saddle. She fought and struggled but Jimmy just laughed and smacked her on her muddy backside as he wheeled his horse around and cantered back to Cameron with a triumphant grin.

"I fetched her for ye—yeeeowww!" He broke off with a yell of pain. He stared down at the girl in shock. "She bit me! The wee vixen bit me!"

The wee vixen moved to bite his leg again and Jimmy hastily shoved her off his horse. She dropped lightly to the ground and glanced warily around, preparing to run again.

"There's no need to be a'feared," Cameron said hastily. He dismounted and took a few slow steps toward her, holding up his hands pacifically, saying in a soothing voice, "Nobody here will harm you. My cousin is a wee bit enthusiastic, that's all—"

"He's drunk," the girl said, backing away.

"Maybe, but he meant well," Cameron told her.

She snorted. "Meant well? To kidnap me in broad daylight?"

"Nobody's going to kidnap you," Cameron assured her softly and moved closer. She backed away and glanced at the bog, as if weighing her chances of escaping across it.

"Ye daft wee besom, he wants tae marry you," Jimmy said, still rubbing his leg.

She snorted. "He's drunker than I thought."

It was now or never, Cameron thought. He cleared his throat. "It's true," he said. It came out as a croak.

She made a gesture of disgust. "You're drunk, too.

"I'm not. It's true, I'm offering you marriage." There, it was out. He was officially crazy. But at least he'd get control of his inheritance.

Away on the moors a curlew called, a mournful, other-worldly cry. The wind blew across the bog, carrying the scent of heather and dank, rotting mud.

Chapter Three

THE GIRL SCRUTINIZED his face, then turned to look at each of his cousins. "Marriage?" she said eventually. "You're proposing marriage to me? To *me*?"

Cameron nodded. "Aye."

In her dirty, mud-streaked face, her blue eyes gleamed bright with suspicion. "Why?"

Cameron shrugged. "I must marry someone. Why not you?" It was ridiculous when said aloud, but with the eyes of his cousins on him, he wasn't going to back down. He'd never broken his word yet.

But he might not have to. The girl could still refuse. He waited.

Down the road the girl's sheepdog barked. A sheep baaed in response. "You're tetched in the head," she told him. "You canna mean such a thing. Why, you never set eyes on me before today."

"It sounds mad, I know, but it's an honest offer I'm making ye," Cameron told her.

Stunned, Jeannie McLeay chewed on her lip and stared at the solemn young man in front of her. He was asking her to marry him? It couldn't possibly be true. He probably wouldn't even recognize her if he met her again—she was all over mud, anyway. He was drunk, or tetched in the head, but . . . Marriage? The thought gave her pause.

She would have married almost anyone to get away from Grandad and the sheep. And suddenly, like something out of a dream, here was this tall, beautiful young man, asking her.

Was he one of the fairy folk? She'd never believed in them—well, not since she was a little girl—but she'd heard they were invariably beautiful, and this one certainly qualified.

He'd wiped his face clean of mud. His cheekbones and jaw might have been cut with a blade, they were so perfect and sharp. His nose was bold and straight as a sword and his mouth firm and unsmiling. And his chin . . . Her mother always used to say a man with a firm chin could be relied on.

Warrior stock, no doubt, like many folk in the highlands, of Viking descent. His hair was brown and sun-streaked, yet his eyes weren't Viking blue, but hazel. They watched her steadily, but she sensed an intensity beneath the calm manner.

And going by the quality of his clothes and his horse he was not exactly poor.

God knew why he'd even looked twice at her, with her in her grandad's old coat and boots and covered in mud, but he had. And try as she might, she could not dismiss it. She pinched herself, hard, to be sure it wasn't a dream.

"I don't know you from Adam," she said to silence the clamor in her head.

"My name is Cameron Fraser."

Fraser. It was a common enough name around here.

Oh Lord. She ought not to even consider his proposal. The poor lad was no doubt a wee bit soft in the head, and his friends were too drunk to realize what he was doing.

But she was only human.

The choices loomed large in her head; life with her grandfather, the stingiest, gloomiest, dourest man in all of Scotland, or life with this tall, solemn young man.

The rest of her life spent on the moors, half the time cold, wet and hungry, looking after Grandad's sheep, or marriage to this beautiful young man who was probably tetched in the head to be offering marriage to her on so little acquaintance.

No choice at all.

People said better the devil you knew. Not Jeannie.

"Do ye have a house?" she asked.

"I do."

"Would I be its mistress?" It was the summit of her dreams—to have a home of her own, to be beholden to no-one. To belong.

He nodded. "My mother died when I was a bairn. You'd be the woman of the house."

The woman of the house. There it was, her dream laid out for her. All she had to do was to say yes. She swallowed. What if he proved to be a madman or violent?

She thought of how he'd plunged into the bog and hauled her and the sheep out. He hadn't given a thought to his fine clothes. And he'd set the lamb on its feet with a gentle hand.

No, he wasn't a violent man, and if she was wrong, well, she was fleet of foot and nimble. She could always run away. She'd been planning to run away from Grandad anyway, only she hadn't yet worked out how to do it without a bean to her name and nowhere to run to. A different situation would offer different opportunities.

A home of her own. The woman of the house. Not like she was now, an indigent relative but treated like a servant, taken in begrudgingly and reminded of it daily.

Her own home. And a place of honor in it as his wife.

It was probably a joke. He was making a May game of her, but oh, oh, if it were true. Mad or tetched or drunk, he was young and beautiful and the thought of those lithe, powerful limbs wrapping around her made her shiver.

She gazed into his eyes, trying to read his mind. Steady hazel eyes met hers, telling her nothing. But they were steady, not wild.

She moistened her lips and took the plunge. "Ye truly mean it?"

"I do." He gave a curt nod to emphasize it.

He sounded sincere. He looked sincere. Oh God, let him be sincere, she prayed.

She took a deep breath. "Well then, I'll marry you."

The man who'd tried to kidnap her gave a loud whoop, causing his horse to toss its head and plunge restlessly. "She said yes! I win! Pay up, Donald!"

His words punched into Jeannie's gut. All the breath left her lungs. It was a joke after all. A bet. See if you could get the gullible girl to believe a strange man would offer her marriage.

And the fool girl had believed. Had even allowed herself to hope. After all she'd been through in the last few years, had she learned nothing?

She tried to look as if she'd known it all along, as if disappointment and humiliation weren't about to choke her. "A bet, was it, lads? A laugh at my expense?" she said with an attempt at breezy uncon-cern. "Very funny. Enjoy your winnings. I'm awa' then to my sheep." She turned away so they would not see the hot tears prickling at her eyelids.

A firm hand wrapped gently around her elbow, holding her back. "It wasn't a joke," he told her. "There was a bet, yes, but my cousins will bet on anything and everything."

Jeannie stared down at his mud-caked boots, angry and ashamed. The apparent sincerity in his voice confused and angered her. She refused to be caught a second time.

"I meant it," he went on. "And you said you'd wed me."

She jerked her arm away. She wouldn't be made a fool of twice. "As if you'd marry a girl like me, a girl you don't even know. And as if I'd marry a man on an acquaintance of five minutes."

"You said you would."

She made a rude noise. "I was only going along with the joke. Why would I want to marry a man I'd just met?"

"Perhaps because you're desperate—"

She looked up at him then, glaring, ready to spit in his eye.

"Maybe even as desperate as I am," he finished.

His words stopped her cold. "You? Desperate?" she managed after a moment. "Why would you be desperate?"

"I need to gain control of my inheritance. My uncle—my trustee—is spending it like water. I inherit when I turn thirty, or when I wed. If I wait much longer there'll be nothing left."

Jeannie turned his words over in her mind, then

shook her head. "You're saying you're to be rich? But there's nobody else you can marry? Only a girl you fished from a bog?"

"There are plenty of other girls," he admitted. "But I swore I'd marry the first woman I met. And that was you."

Marry the first woman he met? Jeannie couldn't believe her ears. She glanced at his cousins who sat on their horses, watching wide-eyed, like great gormless owls, to see what would happen next.

"Is this true?" she demanded. They nodded.

"You'd truly marry a stranger, just to get your hands on your inheritance?"

"I said I would and I never break my word," he said.

"He never breaks his word," the cousins chorused.

"That's the daftest thing I've ever heard," she said.

He shrugged. "Maybe. So, will you marry me?"

Jeannie stared into the steady hazel eyes, trying to read his true intent. She could read nothing, so she looked away into the distance, trying to decide what to do. She could smell the mud on her, feel it tightening on her skin as it dried. She must look a sight.

"I give you my word I'll take good care of you, Jeannie McLeay."

His word. The one he never broke. And he had big, broad, lovely shoulders, even if he was cracked in the head. "When?" she asked.

"Today."

Jeannie closed her eyes, counted to ten, and then counted again, just to make sure. And then she tossed commonsense to the wind. "All right, I'll do it. Where do we go?"

"The nearest kirk. St Andrew's-by-the-burn?"

She nodded. It was the closest church, though

Grandad wasn't a believer and she'd never been allowed to attend.

Cameron Fraser mounted his horse and held out his hand to help her up behind him.

She hesitated and glanced back at the sheep waiting in a close huddle at the end of the causeway. Rab, the sheepdog, lay quietly, watching her, watching the sheep, ever vigilant.

Cameron Fraser followed her gaze. "If you want, Jimmy will stay to take care of your sheep."

She looked skeptically at the cousin who swayed on his horse, grinning muzzily. "They'll be safer wi' the dog. Have ye a handkerchief?"

He handed her a clean, folded handkerchief, no doubt thinking she meant to clean herself with it. The state she was in, she was beyond one handkerchief.

She picked up a stone, plucked a sprig of heather growing by the side of the road and knotted them both into the handkerchief. Then she let out a shrill whistle. The dog raced toward her like a dart.

She tied the handkerchief onto his collar. "I'll miss ye, Rab," she whispered, stroking the dog's silky ears. He'd been the only source of love and affection she'd had in six long years. She'd miss him, but Rab would be all right with Grandad. Her grandfather was a lot kinder to animals than he was to people.

"Away home wi' them, Rab," she said. "Away home." The dog raced back and began to circle the sheep. A bark here, a nip there and the herd began to move. They'd be home soon.

"Will no-one worry when the sheep come home without you?" Cameron Fraser asked her.

"No. Grandad will understand the message in the handkerchief. He won't be troubled, as long as no sheep are missing, and Rab will get them home safe."

It was the exact same message her mother had left when she ran off with her father more than twenty years ago. Mam had left a stone, a sprig of heather and a note. A stone for Grandad's heart, and heather for Mam's hopes for the future. Jeannie had no paper for a note, but Grandad would remember.

He frowned. "But he'll want to know where you've gone, surely."

Clearly it didn't reflect well on her that she had no-one who cared. Jeannie tried to pass it off with a laugh. "He'll be relieved to have me off his hands."

Cameron Fraser quirked a brow at her. "Trouble, are you?"

"Aye, I eat too much and I'm the worst shepherdess he's ever had."

He smiled for the first time, and it was as bright as the sun reflecting off the silvery loch. It set off a flutter deep inside her.

"He never wanted me in the first place. I was dumped on him when my mother died six years ago." Lord, she was babbling. She bit her tongue.

"From now on, you can eat what you like, and you'll never have to look after sheep again." He held out his hand.

"I'd marry the devil himself for that promise." She took hold of Cameron Fraser's hand, swung up behind him and, heart in her mouth, rode off to meet her fate.

Chapter Four

THE SMALL STONE kirk of St. Andrew's-by-the-burn was the last remnant of a hamlet that was slowly dying. The elderly minister and his wife were in the front garden, tending to the rose bushes.

"Good day to ye, Reverend." Cameron dropped lightly to the ground, placed his hands around Jeannie McLeay's waist and lifted her down.

"Cameron Fraser, is it you?" The minister came forward, brushing twigs and leaves from his clothes.

"Aye, Reverend, it is. I hope you and Mrs. Potts are well." Cameron was well aware of the minister's shrewd gaze running over them all, noting his cousins' inebriation, his own muddy state, and finally coming to rest on the muddy scrap he'd just helped dismount.

"And what is it ye want of me, Cameron? This is no' a social call I'll be thinking."

"I need you to perform a marriage." Cameron said it briskly, as if there was nothing at all strange in such a request. He held a hand out to the scrap and drew her to his side. "This is Miss Jeannie McLeay, originally of the Island of Lewis, and we are betrothed."

There was a muffled sound from the minister's wife, but the man himself didn't turn a hair.

Cameron continued, "We wish to be married today. Now, in fact."

The minister frowned. "No banns?"

"If ye can't do it now, just say so and we'll go elsewhere," Cameron said calmly. He'd prefer a church wedding, but Scottish laws ensured he didn't need the minister's cooperation. A declaration before witnesses would do it, and the minister knew it.

He eyed Jeannie dubiously. "Are ye of age, Miss McLeay?"

"I'm nineteen," she said, sounding quite composed for a girl with half a bog on her.

The minister pursed his lips. "Very well, then. I suppose I should be glad you've come to the kirk for it. Better a marriage with God's blessing than some godless arrangement. Come ye in. We'll get the details down. I expect they'll be glad of a cup of tea, Elspeth."

"Indeed, indeed," his wife said, looking curiously at the girl behind Cameron.

Cameron made to lead the scrap into the minister's house, but she didn't budge.

"I'm no' going into the house, not like this." She gestured at her muddy garments. She turned to the minister's wife. "Would it be possible for me to wash around the back of the house, ma'am?"

The minister's wife brightened. "Of course, my dear. I can see you've had a nasty encounter with some mud. Come along with me." She held her gestured to the path around the side of the house.

The minister waited until they'd disappeared from sight and then said, "Now Cameron, you'd better tell me what kind of a mess you've got yourself in this time."

"I'm not in a mess, Reverend Potts," Cameron said

stiffly. The man was some kind of distant relation but it didn't excuse his familiarity.

The minister's brows rose skeptically. "Not in a mess? And yet you turn up out of the blue demanding to be wed to a lass who's mud to the eyebrows, here and now, no banns, no witnesses except for those feckless young wastrels."

The feckless young wastrels made indignant noises, but Rev. Potts swept on, "And none of the celebrations that one would expect of the wedding of the laird."

"None of that matters," Cameron told him. "Just wed us and be done."

Reverend Potts put a hand on Cameron's arm. "What is it, lad? Has the girl trapped you into this?"

Cameron shook off his hand. "She has not. And I don't propose to discuss it. If you're not willing to marry us, then say so and we'll be off."

The minister took a step back. "Now, now, laddie, no need to be like that. As long as you're happy about it, I'll wed the pair of ye, and gladly." He glanced down at Cameron's muddy breeches and boots. "But you'll not want to be married wi' your boots and breeks in such a state."

"It doesna matter——" Cameron began.

"It's not respectful to your bride to be married in dirt," the minister went on inexorably. "Come ye in and get cleaned up."

She was in an even muddier state, Cameron thought, but he followed the man anyway. He could at least clean up for her, he supposed.

———∾———

In the large, cozy kitchen at the back of the house, Elspeth Potts and her cook were firmly stripping Jeannie of her muddy clothes. "Och, child, ye canna go to your wedding reeking of the bog, I'd never forgive myself," Elspeth said. "There's plenty of hot water, so you just climb into the tub there and scrub it all off. Your hair, too — Morag, beat up an egg."

"An egg?" Jeannie's stomach rumbled.

"Aye, followed by a vinegar rinse. T'will give your hair a lovely glossy finish. Now hop in, my dear, before you get cold."

With the last of her clothes stripped from her shivering body, Jeannie had no alternative but to climb into the tin bathtub. She'd been prepared to scrub the worst of it off with a bucket of cold water, but Mrs. Potts wouldn't hear of it. "Cold water? Nonsense. A bride deserves the best we can give her, isn't that right, Morag?"

So Jeannie luxuriated in a tub of warm water and scrubbed the dirt from her body. The bath water was soon black and the minister's wife ordered a second bath, with hotter water. This time, instead of the strong-smelling soap Jeannie had used the first time, she gave her a small oval cake that smelled of roses.

"It's beautiful," Jeannie said, inhaling the rich scent as she lathered her body for the second time.

"It's French," the older lady admitted. "A terrible indulgence for a minister's wife, but I confess, I cannot resist it. Now, close your eyes and Morag will shampoo your hair with the egg."

It seemed a waste of good food, but Jeannie sat in the deep tin bath with her eyes closed while Mrs. Potts and Morag fussed over her. The hot water was blissful. For the last six years she'd bathed in water that was barely luke-warm: Grandad's kettle only held a small amount of hot water and he didn't approve of wasting fuel to heat water for baths.

She felt herself relaxing as Morag's strong fingers massaged her scalp. It was so long since anyone had seemed to care if she lived or died, let alone felt clean and smelled good. Six years since Mam had died but now, with her eyes closed, she could almost believe Mam was here, helping prepare her for her wedding.

She stood while Morag rinsed her down like a child, wrapped her in a large towel and then rinsed her hair carefully, several times, with water, then vinegar, then with a mixture that also smelled of roses.

"There you go, lassie, sit ye down by the fire now and drink this." Morag pushed a cup of hot, sweet tea into her hand. Jeannie drank it gratefully.

She dried her hair by the fire, using her fingers to untangle it. The pile of muddy clothes lay on the stone floor where she'd discarded them and her heart sank. Not much use in being clean and sweet-smelling when the only clothes she had were muddy cast-offs. The dresses she'd brought to Grandad's six years ago were long outgrown or worn out. The skirt she'd worn today was a patched together creation of what remained of them. But she had no choice. She'd have to dry her clothes by the fire and brush off as much mud as she could.

"Here you are," Mrs. Potts swept into the room with an armful of clothes. "We'll find something pretty for you here."

"But—"

"Hush now, I can see you've lost your own clothes, and I'll not let a bride be wed in those." She flapped disdainful fingers toward the muddy pile. "Now, let's see." She pulled out a couple of dresses, held them up, shook her head and tossed them on a chair. "Ah, this one, I think. Matches your bonny blue eyes." She held up a dress in soft blue fabric, glanced at Morag for confirmation, and nodded. "Now, let's get you dressed."

She handed Jeannie a bundle of underclothes: a chemise and petticoat in fine, soft lawn, edged with lace, finer than anything Jeannie had worn in her life.

"But I canna accept—" Jeannie began, pride warring with longing for the pretty things.

"Pish tush, they're old things I have no more use for. They don't even fit me now, see?" Mrs. Potts patted her rounded shape comfortably. She added in a softer voice, "And it would give me great pleasure, Jeannie McLeay, to know that you go to your wedding dressed as a bride should be, from the skin out. You've a handsome young man there who'll appreciate them later." She winked. "Come now, indulge an old woman."

Blushing and wordless at the unexpected kindness, Jeannie donned the chemise and petticoat. She picked up the stockings and looked up in shock. "These are silk."

Mrs. Potts flapped her fingers at her. "Well of course—silk for a bridal. Besides, what use are silk stockings for an old woman like me? Now, no argument. And try these slippers on." She handed Jeannie a pair of soft brown leather slippers.

They were a bit big for Jeannie, but once Morag had stuffed the toes with wool, they fitted well enough.

"Now for your hair."

Jeannie began to twist it in a rope around her hand.

"No, no, no! Leave it out. 'Tis your glory, child, and as a married woman you'll be covering it up soon enough. In the meantime leave it out to dazzle that man of yours."

Jeannie wasn't sure she had it in her to dazzle anyone—she was no beauty, she knew — but if Mrs. Potts said her hair could dazzle, Jeannie would leave it out.

She had no idea what marriage to Cameron Fraser would be like, but she would do her best to make it work. And kind Mrs. Potts was giving her a head start.

Producing a brush, Mrs. Potts brushed out Jeannie's long hair till it shone, then produced a veil of creamy, precious lace, which she placed carefully over Jeannie's head. "'Twas my own bridal veil, and both my daughters wore it at their weddings, too."

She stood back and smiled. "There, a bonny bride you are indeed, is she not Morag? Right now, I'll just—" She broke off, hesitated, then said, "Child, do you have no kith or kin to stand up with you?"

Jeannie shook her head. "There's only Grandad Leith, and he wouldna come. He doesna like people."

Mrs. Potts and Morag exchanged glances. "Would that be Ewen Leith, the one they call 'the hermit'?"

Jeannie nodded. "My mother's father."

"I never realized he had a young girl living with him. I'm sorry lass, if I'd known you were alone up there in the hills, I would have visited."

Jeannie shrugged awkwardly. "It doesna matter."

The older lady hugged her. "Well, you'll not be lonely any longer with young Cameron Fraser for a husband. I'm amazed you two ever met, let alone had time to court. Right then, I'll away and see if the men are ready. Take her to the church door, Morag, and

when you hear the music send her down the aisle."
The minister's wife bustled away.

Jeannie and Morag looked at each other. "Could I
maybe. . . " Jeannie began. "Is there a looking glass
somewhere, so that I could see. . ."

"Och, of course, lass." Morag looked out into the
hallway, then beckoned.

Jeannie stood in front of the looking glass in the
hall and stared. Other than in a pool of water, she
hadn't seen her reflection in six years. Grandad didn't
believe in wasting money on vanity.

She'd changed in that time. Grown up. "I . . . I
look like my mother," she whispered. "I look . . ."
Pretty, she thought. She couldn't say it aloud. Vanity
was a sin. But she thought it and the thought gave
her a warm glow. She was still a bit freckled and
skinny, and her cheeks were red from the cold, and
her mouth too wide and she still had that crooked
tooth but she looked . . . nice. Like a proper bride. A
real bride. She adjusted the beautiful lace veil. If not
for Mrs. Potts's kindness . . .

Emotion surged up in her and her eyes filled with
tears.

"Now stop that, lassie, or you'll start me off as
well," Morag said briskly. "Time enough for tears
later. Let's get ye to the kirk."

Chapter Five

THEY WAITED IN the vestibule of the small stone kirk until they heard the full chord of an organ sound. Jeannie took a deep breath. One step and she was on her way to wed Cameron Fraser, a man she'd known but a few hours. And once married there was no going back.

She couldn't move.

"Go on, lass," Morag whispered and gave her a hefty shove that sent her stumbling into the aisle.

And there he was, waiting. Cameron Fraser, solemn as a judge and as fine a man as she'd ever seen. To her surprise he wore the kilt, the Fraser dress kilt, a splash of bright color in the austere little whitewashed kirk.

Jeannie's heart fluttered. She'd always been partial to the sight of a man wearing the kilt. And Cameron Fraser looked as braw and bonny as any man she'd seen. The man had a set of legs on him that fair took her breath away.

The music continued and Jeannie walked slowly down the aisle, drinking in the sight of her groom. He wore a white shirt with a lace jabot at his throat, the foam of the lace in stark contrast to the hard line of his jaw and square, firm chin. Over it he wore a black velvet coat with silver buttons. He looked like a hero out of a painting of old.

His expression hadn't changed. He looked . . . No, she couldn't read his face at all. He ran a finger between his throat and his jabot, as if it was tied too tight.

Was he having second thoughts?

She hoped not because she wanted him, wanted him with a fierceness that burned bright and deep within her. She quickened her step.

Cameron Fraser had made her want him. He'd caused all her long buried dreams to surface, had tantalized her with possibilities she knew were foolish and impossible, but now she wanted him, wanted the house he'd promised her, the place, the home. Her home. And him. She wanted it all.

He was not going to back out now. She hurried the last few steps to where he waited at the altar and when he presented his arm, she grabbed it. And held on tight.

He stared down at her, looking faintly stunned.

Cameron couldn't believe his eyes. This was his muddy little bog sprite? This lissom young woman walking toward him with shining eyes and a look of hope so transparent it went straight to his heart.

Behind him, one of his cousins said something but Cameron wasn't listening. His attention was entirely on his bride as she made the interminable walk down the aisle, light and graceful in a pretty blue dress.

He straightened, glad now he'd stuffed his kilt and jacket into his saddlebag when he left, glad the minister had insisted it wouldn't do for the laird to be wed in his breeks, even if nobody except a couple of young wastrels were there to witness it. His bride would remember he'd done her honor on this day, the old man had said.

Cameron ran a finger around his neck. He hadn't wanted the fussy lace jabot. The minister had pressed it on him at the last moment, completing the full formal dress.

Cameron was glad of it now. His bride was . . . He took a deep breath and faced it: his bride, his little bog sprite, was beautiful. Not the perfect, polished beauty in the portraits of his mother, nor the ripe, sensual beauty of Ailine, the widow who'd first taught a brash boy how to please a woman.

Jeannie McLeay's beauty was something quite different.

She was the scent of heather on the wind, the softness of mist in the glen, and the clean, fresh air of the mountains. It was a subtle beauty, like that of his homeland, not delicate and whimsical and demanding as his mother had been, but strong and free and bonny.

She wore a softly draped veil of lace over long, glossy chestnut hair that fell clear to her waist. Where had she hidden that hair? His fingers itched to run through the silken length of it. Her skin was smooth and fresh with a dozen or so small freckles, like brown breadcrumbs sprinkled over cream, her cheeks a wild rose blush echoed in her soft, full lips.

Cameron straightened under his bride's clear gaze. She liked how he looked too, he could tell by the feminine approval in her wide blue eyes. He drew himself up, glad now he'd worn the kilt and even the stupid, fussy jabot.

She gazed up at him, clinging tightly to his arm, and gave him a hesitant, shy, faintly anxious smile that pierced his heart.

His bride.

"Dearly beloved."

They turned and faced the minister. It passed in a blur. Cameron heard himself making his vows. His bride spoke hers in a clear, soft voice.

"Time to sign the register," the minister said. He handed Cameron the pen. Cameron signed it and passed it to his bride.

She took it, but made no move to sign. Her thoughts seemed far away.

Of course, she wouldn't know how to read or write, he realized, and his stomach hollowed as he took in the implications of his rash act.

"Dip the end in the ink and make your mark," Cameron told her in a low voice. "A cross will do. Or a thumbprint if you prefer."

She gave him an odd look, then dipped the quill in the ink and swiftly wrote her name in a stylish copperplate hand.

Cameron blinked. How had a simple shepherdess learned to write like that?

He was still pondering that question while the minister recited some advice about marriage. And then the words, "You may kiss the bride."

Cameron lifted the veil back off her face. To his surprise, his hands were shaking. She turned her face up to him, her eyes shining, trustful, her lips rosy, slightly parted.

He stared down at her. This thing he'd done so carelessly, this marriage he'd made without consideration, thinking only of his inheritance: it had become something momentous. This girl had given herself into his care, forever. She was his.

He bent and touched his mouth to hers, intending to make it brief, but her lips softened under his and she sighed and leant into him, and before he knew it he was kissing her deeply, his senses swimming with the taste, the scent and the feel of her.

"That's enough for now, lad," the minister's voice cut in dryly. "Save the rest for the honeymoon."

Cameron released her, dazed, still hungry. He stared at her in shock. She blinked up at him, blushing, a little disheveled, her mouth soft and moist, her eyes dreamy.

His wife.

Afterward, they returned to the minister's house for tea. "It's not much of a wedding breakfast, I'm afraid," Mrs. Potts said, "but it's the best Morag and I can do at such short notice, and it'll keep you going until you get home."

"It's very fine thank you, Mrs. Potts," Cameron assured her, and indeed the minister's wife had put on a feast. There was shortbread and egg-and-bacon tart and Selkirk bannock and warm, fresh-baked baps with butter and honey. And if Cameron and his cousins thought it a poor celebration to be washing such fine food down with tea instead of whisky, they knew better than to say so. Not in front of a minister.

Not that Cameron cared. He was watching his bride eat her way through every piece of food offered her with an expression of utter bliss.

Halfway through a slice of Selkirk bannock, she set it down with a huge, regretful sigh. "I'm sorry, but I canna eat a single mouthful more. It's the most delicious meal I've had in forever, Mrs. Potts, Morag." She laughed. "Grandad thinks porridge is all a body needs."

He recalled that her grandfather had claimed she ate too much. She was as slender as a reed.

Cameron stood. "We'd best get along home now. Thank you for all you've done, Reverend Potts, Mrs. Potts, Morag." He bowed to each. "You've turned this into a very special occasion."

At his words, Jeannie jumped up. "Oh, your dress," she said to Mrs. Potts. "I should change back into—"

The older woman shook her head. "Keep the dress my dear, with my blessing. And here's a wee wedding present for you." She gave Jeannie a parcel wrapped in brown paper. "Open it tonight, before you go to bed."

For the sake of politeness Jeanie made a few half-hearted protests but she was glad to leave her old clothes—and her old life—behind. She hugged the motherly minister's wife and thanked her again.

Then it was time to mount up again, this time with Jeannie riding in front of Cameron, seated side-ways across his saddle because the blue dress was too narrow-cut to allow for sitting astride—not with-out a scandalous amount of leg showing. Jeannie was made comfortable enough with a cushion borrowed from Mrs. Potts and in a short time they were off and heading toward her new home.

With her new husband. The thought took her breath away. It was like a dream. His arms were wrapped around her, holding her steady, warm and strong. Her husband.

Chapter Six

THEY BREASTED A hill and stopped to take in the view. A rocky promontory jutted deep into the sea where a castle loomed, gloomy and forbidding. A village nestled at its foot, a scattering of neat cottages—or largely neat. Quite a few had damaged roofs.

Jeannie eyed them eagerly. One of those cottages would be hers. She couldn't wait. "Which house is yours?"

"The big one." He pointed.

Two cottages were larger than the others. One was on the outskirts of the village and the other was in the centre, facing the village square. Both had intact roofs, she was glad to see. "Is it the one in the town or the one next to the wee burn," she asked. She didn't mind which.

"Neither of those. The big one," he repeated.

"But—" She broke off. Did he mean. . .? "You don't mean . . . *the castle?*" Her voice came out in a squeak.

"Aye."

She twisted in the saddle to look him in the eye. "Are you some kind of servant?"

He grinned and shook his head.

Jeannie swallowed. "You mean to say you live in the—" She could see the answer in his eyes. He did. "But you said I'd be the woman of the house."

"You will."

"What job do you do in the castle?"

He just grinned. His cousins who, once out of sight of the minister, had recovered their high spirits, guffawed. "He's the laird, lassie," Donald told her. "And you're the laird's wife."

"From the moment you married him," Jimmy added helpfully.

"The laird's wife?" she echoed faintly. A hollow opened up in her. "You mean to say I'll be in charge of that, that enormous place?"

Her husband smiled down at her, pleased at her amazement. "Aye."

They all beamed at her, as if it was some huge treat to be put in charge of a castle with no warning. Or training. Or even any clothes.

She thumped him on the shoulder, hard. "Why didn't you tell me?"

He gave her a bemused look and rubbed his shoulder. "Would it have made any difference?"

"Yes! No—I don't know. You should have warned me." Oh Lord, *the laird's wife.*

"What good would it have done?"

She thumped him again. "I could have prepared myself."

"Clothes, ye mean?" he asked cautiously.

"No, ye great thick-head! Where would I get clothes?" She tapped her forehead. "I mean up here. You told me I'd be mistress in my own home—"

"Well you will be—"

"Not *the laird's wife!*"

"It's the same thing."

She went to thump him again and he caught her fist, laughing.

"It's not the same thing," she said crossly. "A woman in her own cottage answers to nobody. A laird's wife answers to *everyone*. Everyone will have an opinion, from your uncle to the lowest scullery-maid. And if they don't think I'm up to the job—and they'll see at once that I'm no fine high-born lady—they won't respect me, and they won't obey me. Oh, they'll pretend to and be sweet as pie to the mistress's face but they'll resent me and the work will be done shoddily and—"

"For a shepherdess, you seem to know a lot about how a big house runs."

"I've only been a shepherdess for six years," she told him impatiently. "Before that my mother was the housekeeper of a great house. She took the position after my father died and left us with no money. So believe me when I say—"

"Housekeeper?" he interrupted. "Of a great house?"

"Aye, and she—"

"Then you'll know fine how to run a castle, won't ye?" he said, leaving her dumbfounded. He gave a pleased nod and, still holding her fist in one large hand, he urged his horse down the slope toward the castle.

Jeannie swallowed. She wanted to hit him again for being so unreasonably blithe about the problems she faced, but somehow his confidence seeped slowly into her. She did know a little about running a grand house. From the wrong end of things, but still . . .

Besides, she had no choice. She was wedded.

She could do this, she could. As long as nobody

found out he'd fished his bride from a bog, she just might be able to pull it off.

Her confidence seeped away as the castle loomed closer. And larger. They trotted over a bridge and through an archway and came to a halt in a courtyard.

Grooms ran out to take the reins of the horses. Cameron Fraser—she had to stop thinking of him by his full name; he was her husband now, not a stranger—*Cameron* dismounted and lifted Jeannie down. She stretched her cramped limbs in relief, shook her crumpled skirts out and tidied her hair as best she could.

"Ready?" Cameron asked her.

She wasn't, she wanted to run in the opposite direction, but she nodded, and without warning he swept her into his arms and carried her up the steps to the great iron-studded oak door.

"What—?"

"Stop struggling. It's tradition. Carry the bride over the threshold," he said. His cousins ran ahead and banged loudly on the door, shouting that the laird had brought home a bride. As they reached it the door swung open. Cameron strode through it.

Jeannie clung to his neck, gazing around her, trying to look graceful and composed. Her stomach was a battlefield of demented butterflies.

People came from everywhere, popping out of doorways and flowing down stairs, staring at her, crowding in after Cameron, flocking to see the laird's bride, laughing and clapping and buzzing with surprised speculation.

"He married the first woman he found," Jimmy shouted exuberantly to the crowd. "Fished her out of a muddy bog and married her!"

Jeannie's fingers curled into fists. "I'm going to kill your cousin," she muttered into Cameron's neck.

He laughed. "Best it's out from the beginning. You're my wife, nothing can change that."

"I'm still going to kill him."

Cameron carried her into a room he said was called the Great Hall. It was a big, barren-looking room, all gray stone and dark wooden beams and paneling, with an ancient fireplace as big as a horse stall.

Cameron set her carefully on her feet, took her hand and raised it. "Meet your new mistress, formerly Jeannie McLeay of the Isle of Lewis, now Jeannie McLeay Fraser, the Lady of Roskirk."

Jeannie blinked. *The Lady of Roskirk?*

Cameron continued, "And I am now officially laird of this estate."

There was a roar of approval and clapping. Jeannie was under no illusion that the approval was for her. It was Cameron they were cheering, and that he was, at last, their laird.

They came forward to be introduced, one by one, first relatives, of whom there were a surprising number, then members of the household. Jeannie tried to remember the names but they soon became a blur.

Of her husband's newly deposed trustee uncle, there was no sign.

"And this is the housekeeper, Mrs. Findlay," Cameron said.

Mrs. Findlay was a tall, dour-looking, middle-aged woman. Dressed entirely in pristine grey, with her steel-gray hair pulled back in a severe bun, she looked crisp, efficient and unfriendly.

Facing her, Jeannie felt tired and crumpled and inadequate, but everyone was watching and she would not be intimidated. She inclined her head pleasantly. "Mrs. Findlay."

The housekeeper curtseyed and handed her a large bunch of keys on a round metal circlet, saying stiffly, "The keys to the household, my lady. As the Lady of Roskirk, they are yours by right."

The ring of keys weighed heavily in Jeannie's hand. Her mother had carried just such a collection on her belt. She took a deep breath, praying it was the right thing to do, and handed them back to the housekeeper, saying in a clear voice, "Thank you Mrs. Findlay, but I'm sure you know what to do with these, much better than I do at the moment. I learned something of the running of a great house from my mother, of course, but I'm a new bride and still have much to learn." She smiled and added, "I can see for myself the castle is well run. I hope we'll work well together."

There was an almost audible sigh in the room as the housekeeper took the keys back, saying, "I'm sure we will, my lady. If it's convenient, I could show you the house and its workings tomorrow."

Jeannie nodded. "That would be very convenient, thank you."

As the housekeeper turned away, Cameron slipped Jeannie's hand in his and squeezed it briefly. "Well done."

She felt a small glow of satisfaction, and as the rest of the household came up to be introduced, she addressed them with growing confidence.

Suddenly a hush fell. The crowd parted and a tall, white haired gentleman came slowly forward. It wasn't his hair, but a white-powdered wig, she saw as he came closer. Wearing silk knee breeches, high

heeled shoes with glittering ruby buckles and a lav-
ishly embroidered coat and waistcoat, the man still
affected the fashions of a bygone era.

"Uncle Charles," Cameron murmured, though
she'd already guessed that from everyone's reactions.

Cameron introduced them stiffly, poised, Jeannie
saw, to defend her from any insult his uncle might
direct at her. The realization warmed her.

Uncle Charles, however, behaved like the perfect courtier, in manner as well as in dress. Bowing
gracefully over Jeannie's hand he murmured, "Welcome to Roskirk, my lady. Congratulations on your
marriage."

He turned to his nephew, and held out a hand,
saying mildly, "I should have known better than to
doubt you, my boy. Frasers always were stubborn
and determined. I hope you don't regret your hasty
marriage." He glanced at Jeannie and added, "She's
a pretty little thing. I hope she's up to her position."

He'd clearly heard how Cameron had met her,
but other than his doubts—which were understand-
able; she had more than a few herself—Jeannie could
detect disappointment but little rancor in his tone.
She glanced at Cameron, to see if she could tell from
his reaction whether his uncle was being hypocriti-
cal or not, but she couldn't tell.

All he said was, "I'll be able to mend the tenants'
roofs now."

His uncle sighed. "And I suppose you'll cancel my
beautiful hangings from France." He pronounced it
'Fronce' with a pronounced French accent.

"I will indeed. This very night."

His uncle sighed again, then turned and walked
slowly back up the stairs.

The watching household waited, but it soon became clear there would be no dramatic scene and, disappointed, people slowly drifted back to their duties.

Chapter Seven

THEY'D ARRIVED NOT long before the dinner hour, and Jeannie had been taken upstairs to wash and tidy herself. She'd just removed her dress, when a knock sounded, and a young woman appeared breathlessly.

"I'm Mairie, m'lady." She bobbed a swift curtsey. "The laird said I'm to be your own personal maid-servant. What would you like me to do?" She was young, a year or two younger than Jeannie from the look of her, with curly brown hair and a sweet expression.

Jeannie wasn't sure what to do with a maidservant—she'd never had anyone wait on her in her life, but at least this girl seemed friendly, and nowhere near as intimidating as the grim-faced housekeeper.

She indicated her dress. "Can you do anything with that? I'll have to wear it to dinner. It's my only dress."

The girl's eyes widened. "Your only—" She broke off, embarrassed. She picked up the dress and shook it out. "Of course, m'lady."

While the maid did her best to neaten the travel-stained dress, Jeannie washed her face and hands and brushed her hair and wound it into a neat coronet, but with no fresh gown to change into, she felt very self-conscious when Cameron came to escort her down to dinner.

When her husband arrived, Mairie slipped discreetly out, leaving them alone. He was dressed formally in the kilt again, though this time without the lace jabot. He still took her breath away.

"I'll need more clothes," she told him. "I have only this one dress to my name."

He nodded. "Wear these tonight." He dug into his sporran and pulled out a worn, flat box. She opened it to find a rope of lustrous, shimmering pearls. "My mother had a lot of jewels, but I'm told pearls are the most suitable for a bride."

He helped her twine them about her neck. They felt cool and heavy and magnificent against her skin, armor against the feelings of inadequacy that only intensified as he led her down the staircase to the great hall, where they were to dine.

A piper sounded, piping the laird and his new bride in to dinner. The sound shivered down Jeannie's spine as she walked on her husband's arm down the stairs. She was now part of an ancient tradition.

Cameron's uncle was to sit at Jeannie's left hand and from the moment she was seated, began to engage her in light, polite conversation.

Bemused, Jeannie responded to his questions as best she could, but far from the personal interrogation she dreaded about her background and upbringing, she soon found he was entirely uninterested in herself and passionate about his plans for silk hangings for the great hall. He'd designed the hangings himself, was sorely disappointed with the cancellation of the order and clearly aimed to enlist her support in changing Cameron's mind.

"Such a barren and gloomy room, is it not? My nephew lacks the refinement to appreciate such things and has, no doubt, already cancelled the order—"

On the other side of her, she felt Cameron stiffen.

"Mr. Sinclair, I'm sorry but it's been a long day. Perhaps we could discuss this at a later date?" It wasn't a lie. She was exhausted. So much had happened. And there was still her wedding night ahead.

The older man acquiesced gracefully. She'd say this for him, he was a courtier to his beautifully manicured fingertips. She could see his point. The hall was rather bleak and gray and could use some brightening, but it didn't have to be expensive silk hangings from Paris.

And she wasn't going to be drawn into a family quarrel on her first day as a bride.

———

"Are you ready?" Cameron stood beside her chair, his hand out, ready to escort her upstairs.

Jeannie's heart beat a rapid tattoo. Her wedding night. She'd been thinking about it all afternoon, and now she knew exactly what she was going to say . . . He wasn't going to be happy about it.

The wine she'd been drinking at dinner tasted suddenly sour in her throat. She'd soon find out what kind of man she'd married.

At the door of her bedchamber—*their* bedchamber—he raised her hand and kissed it. "I'll leave you to get ready. I'll return in half an hour."

She nodded numbly, dread pooling in her stomach at the delay. She wanted it over and done with. She wanted it endlessly delayed.

Her maid waited inside. There was hot water in the jug and a fire blazing in the hearth. A wine decanter and two glasses stood on the table beside the bed. The very large bed. The sheets were turned down, the pillows plumped and waiting.

On the bed lay the brown paper parcel that the minister's wife had given her. She'd forgotten all about it. Someone must have found it in Cameron's saddlebags and brought it up.

She opened it and found a pretty nightgown, a delicate white woolen shawl, a cake of the rose soap and a small china pot. She opened it and sniffed, then dipped a finger in to test it. Face cream. Luscious and smelling faintly of roses. The nightgown was made of fine soft lawn, narrowly pin-tucked and embroidered at the scooped neck with tiny pink roses.

Jeannie hadn't worn anything so pretty to bed in her life. Given what she planned, it would be a waste to wear it tonight but she couldn't resist. Not that she had anything else to wear.

The maid, Mairie, helped her off with her dress and brushed out her hair, then feeling self-conscious, Jeannie sent her away. She washed with the rose soap, creamed her skin from the little china pot, then put on the dainty nightgown. It slipped over her skin like feathers. So light. So insubstantial. Thank goodness for the fire.

She glanced at her reflection in the looking glass and her eyes widened. The nightdress was so fine it was practically transparent. She arranged the shawl around her, but though warm, it was fine and soft and clung lovingly to her shape. Too lovingly.

It would not do at all.

Through the doorway on the right of the bed-chamber lay another small room. She peeked in.

Clothes hanging on hooks, a chest of drawers, boots and shoes neatly lined up. Cameron's dressing room. She searched through it rapidly until she found what she wanted, an old woolen fishing pullover, slightly unraveled at the neck, but clean. She pulled it on. It fell halfway to her knees. Perfect.

There was a knock on the door. He was here. She ran back into the bedchamber and took a flying leap onto the bed, landing on it as the door opened.

Cameron took a deep breath and opened the door. He was about to take his bride and make a wife of her. He couldn't wait. Ever since he'd seen her walking down the aisle of the kirk, since he'd smelled the scent of her and tasted her mouth, his body had throbbed with the knowledge that this was his woman, and that tonight she'd be his.

He smiled. She sat cross legged on the bed, looking as uncertain as a new born lamb. Under his gaze she flushed, and dragged the bedclothes up like a shield, covering her bare legs. And what the hell was she wearing his old pullover for? The room was perfectly warm—he'd ordered the fire himself.

Mind, he had no complaint; she looked very fetching in the shapeless old thing, one thin, bare shoulder sliding out of the loose raveled neck.

He couldn't wait to strip it off her.

She also looked pale and wary and a wee bit nervous. That was as it should be. Brides were nervous. Grooms were not.

Cameron shrugged off his coat. He wasn't the least bit nervous. He was, not to put too fine a point on it, well primed and raring for action. Well, his body was. But tonight, at least, his desires would have to take second place to hers.

He unbuttoned his waistcoat, placed it on top of his coat and loosened the ties at the neck of his shirt. Her eyes were on him, big and wide and dark in the firelight.

Cameron knew his way around a woman's body. He knew fine how to pleasure a woman. He'd gentle his bride and take her slow and easy, bringing her to the business with all the finesse at his fingertips— and that, he flattered himself, was considerable. She'd find pleasure in her marriage bed, he was determined on it. It would make her a more malleable, contented and obedient wife.

He pulled off his boots and, in his stockinged feet, walked toward the bed, smiling.

"Don't come any closer," she warned, her hands held up ready to ward him off.

Aye, she was nervous, all right. "Don't worry, lass, I'll be gentle."

"I said stop!" she repeated. "There's something I need to say to you first."

Cameron sat down on the end of the bed. "Go ahead."

She scooted back, about as far away from him as she could be and still be on the same bed. "I'm no' going to lie down with you tonight," she told him. "Not as a bride."

Bridal jitters. "And why would that be?" Cameron kept his voice quiet and easy, as he would with an unbroken filly. He folded his arms and waited.

She nervously ran her tongue across her lips. His gaze followed the movement hungrily.

"I don't know you."

"Och, you do. I'm your husband," he said with a glimmer of amusement.

"I ken that fine," she flashed, "But we don't know

each other and I won't—I can't lie down wi' a man I don't . . . I've only just . . . You don't know me at all."

"I know enough," he said calmly, "and in the lying down together we will come to know each other better."

She flushed, a wild rose color that set his blood pounding. "What exactly do you know about me?"

Ah, so that was it. She had a past, some secret she was a'feared he'd discover. "I don't care what you've done in the past, Jeannie. Our marriage starts fresh tonight." He slid along the bed toward her.

She shot off the bed. "Not tonight it doesn't. You will listen to me on this, Cameron Fraser!" She stood in front of the fire, her arms folded across the swell of her breasts, her blue eyes sparking. "I'm not ashamed of anything in my past if that's what you're implying, but you've proved my point. You know nothing about me. I'm not simply some female body you pulled from a bog and wed to get your hands on an inheritance. I'm a person, with hopes and dreams and plans of my own. Aye, we're married, but it's not enough."

He frowned. What the devil was she on about? Of course she was a person. He could see that fine through the thin fabric of her night rail, her long, slender legs silhouetted by the firelight, that silky mane of hair gleaming. The blood pooled in his groin, fueling a growing urgency.

But she was saying no, dammit. And for what? "I don't understand. I've given you my name, brought you to my home, introduced you to my family in all honor. What the hell else do you want?"

She narrowed her eyes. "Don't you curse at me, Cameron Fraser." She took a breath and moderated her tone. "I know we're wed and I appreciate the honor you've done me, indeed I do. But if I'm to be a true wife to you, I want . . . I want . . ."

He flung himself off the bed and prowled slowly toward her, his temper on a knife edge. He'd got her measure now. He'd put a stop to this nonsense. "More jewels? Money? What?"

She swallowed. "I want the same as other brides."

"Clothes? A trousseau? I said I'd buy you—"

"I want to be courted."

He came to an abrupt halt. "Courted?" She wanted to be *courted*? By her *husband*?

She nodded. "Only for a wee while. Just until we know each other better. And then I'll feel more comfortable when we, you know." She glanced at the bed.

His anger slowly died. She was in earnest. And he had, after all, only known her for less than a day. He'd taken one look at her in the kirk, fresh from her bath and clad in blue that almost matched her bonny bright eyes, and he'd been ripe to tup her then and there, minister be damned.

But women were different, he knew.

"What would this courtship entail?" He thought he knew. Flowers, little gifts. Pretty speeches. And poetry, he thought gloomily. He hated poetry.

She bit her lip and considered it a moment. "Talking mainly," she said at last. "Getting to know each other. Perhaps a few walks."

It wasn't much to ask. Walking and talking? He could do that. "No poetry then?" he said, cheering up.

Her eyes lit. "Oh yes, that would be lovely. Do you like poetry?"

"No," he said hastily. "I don't know many poems."

A handful of dirty ditties, not fit for her ears. "But I could teach you to ride."

"That would be very nice," she said in the kind of voice that told him she'd prefer he spouted poetry. She waited, with that hopeful look in her eyes that unmanned him every damned time.

Capitulation loomed. "How long would this courting period last?" He didn't like the idea, didn't want to wait for what his body hungered for, but she was his wife and he owed her respect. And he couldn't withstand that damned appealing look.

"A fortnight?"

He sighed. A fortnight? Two whole weeks? Fourteen nights of waiting, unfulfilled? It would probably kill him, especially if he had to look at those legs of hers much longer. But it wasn't an unreasonable request.

"Very well, a fortnight," he agreed. "On one condition."

"What's that?"

"We both sleep in the same bed—this bed. I give you my word I'll do nothing you don't want," he added before she could argue.

Courting couples did a great deal more than talking. Kissing, rolling around in the hay, all kinds of intimate exploration. He'd court her in bed with soft words and caresses. By the end of the fortnight when they came to do the deed she'd be aching for him as he ached for her now.

She gave him a wary look, sensing a trap.

"I don't want people gossiping about our marriage," he said.

"They're already gossiping about it," she pointed out.

"Aye, because it was sudden and unexpected, and

because my idiot cousin spilled the beans about how we met. But if the people of the castle learn the marriage hasna even been consummated—put it this way, they'll no' be speaking kindly of a bride who married their laird then refused to lie down wi' him."

She flushed and in a low voice said, "Oh. I didn't think of that." She swallowed. "Very well, I agree. We sleep in the same bed."

"Right then." Cameron strode to the bed, flipped the covers back, pulled out his *sgian dubh* and cut his forearm. Blood spurted from the cut.

Chapter Eight

"WHAT ARE YOU doing?" Horrified, Jeannie flew across the room to him. Fending her off with one hand, he shook a few drops of blood onto the sheets then turned and allowed her to examine his arm.

She grabbed a clean handkerchief and pressed it to the cut. It didn't look serious but any cut, even a small one, could be dangerous. Da had died of a rose thorn that had festered in his flesh. "What on earth were you thinking of?" She fetched the whisky from the side table.

"It's nothing. Dinna fuss, woman." He sheathed the *sgian dubh*.

"Nothing? You cut yourself deliberately!" She uncorked the bottle and tipped a little whisky onto the cut.

His breath hissed in. It must have stung. Good. "Waste of good whisky," he muttered.

"Even a small wound can fester," she said severely. "Why do such a thing to yourself?"

He shrugged. "I'll not have the maids spreading rumors about your virginity. Or lack of it."

"I don't lack—oh." She broke off in blushing comprehension and stared at the bright stains on the sheet. "You cut yourself for me, to preserve my honor," she whispered.

Jeannie looked at him in wonder. This tall young bridegroom of hers, a man she barely knew—he'd cut himself for her, to protect her from gossip and unkindness. What husband would do that for a bride who'd just refused him her bed? A bride he hardly knew, a bride he'd lifted from *a bog* and raised to the finest position in the district. He'd taken her from poverty and hardship—from misery with Grandad and the sheep—and made her his wife. The *laird's* wife.

Warmth flooded her. He'd given her so much.

She lifted her mouth to his and a kiss that started in gratitude ended in passion. The taste of him entered her blood like hot strong whisky, wild and dark and thrilling, dissolving her doubts, her fears.

The heated demand of his kisses, the leashed desire of his strong, lean body, the salt-clean scent of his skin—it all seemed so right, so familiar to her. How, when it had been barely a day? But time didn't seem to matter, not when she was feeling . . . this.

He grabbed the hem of the pullover and dragged it up. She hesitated.

"It's a scratchy old thing," he murmured. And then he added, "Don't be a'feard of me, lass. You have my word, I'll not do anything you don't want."

Gazing at his mouth, his beautiful, damp, clever mouth, and his steady hazel eyes, she lifted her arms and let him drag the pullover over her head. Cool air caressed her skin and from the way his eyes dropped, she knew her nipples were hard and risen. And aching.

She wanted him. She knew it, and from the look in his eyes, so did he.

Even before he'd tossed the pullover aside she was kissing him again. The taste of him was like wildfire in her blood.

Desperate to touch him she slipped her hands under his shirt, over his chest, caressing the smooth, hard planes, and all the time kissing, kissing . . .

He bent her back over the bed, half lying, grasping her by the hips and positioning her between his long brawny thighs, bare thighs, covered only by the kilt.

Her hands dropped to his waist. She could feel the buckles of his kilt. And beneath the heavy fabric, the hardness of a man, aroused, pressing against her belly in silent, heated demand. She'd never felt it before, but she knew fine what it meant.

All she had to do was say yes, and he'd make her his wife in body as well as name.

Yes? Or no? She teetered on the brink. Cameron had been everything that was kind and honorable. He'd rescued her from life with Grandad, offered her his name and a life she hadn't even dared dream of. He'd even cut his own flesh to protect her good name.

She *owed* him this. And she wanted him.

His big hard body pressed against her, hot and heavy with desire.

Wanting poetry and walks and flowers? Instead of this? Was she mad?

But if she gave in to him now, she knew she'd regret it in the morning.

He'd married her only to get control of his inheritance. He'd known her a bare handful of minutes before he'd proposed marriage. An hour or two later they'd stood before the minister, exchanging vows. And now he had her, as good as naked, in his bed.

Who Jeannie McLeay was, what kind of person she was, what might her fears and hopes and dreams be—none of that had mattered to him in the least. As long as she wasn't related to him and was free to marry—that's all he'd cared about.

Now in the warm, dark night, in a soft feather bed with firelight gilding their limbs, she could have been anyone, any willing girl who'd agreed to marry him and lie in his bed. It wouldn't matter to him.

But Jeannie wanted very much to matter to this man. And for that, she had to make him notice her. Not only her body, but her—a person.

I'll not do anything you don't want. He was a man with a reputation for keeping his vows. She closed her eyes briefly, hoping it was true.

"Cameron?"

"What?" He cupped her breast in his hand and thumbed the nipple gently. She shuddered helplessly.

"S-stop."

"Why? Don't you like it?" His voice was deep, soft. Knowing. His hand kept moving. Shivers of pleasure rippled through her.

"Yes—n—" She dragged in a deep breath. "Y—you said you wouldn't—" She ended on a gasp.

"I said I wouldn't do anything you didn't want." He kissed her. "Do you not want me to do this?" His fingers wandered, leaving trails of heat and desire. "Or this?" He sounded almost amused. As if he knew full well how much she liked it.

He was altogether too sure of her surrender. She took a deep breath, pushed his hand away and tried to wriggle out from under him. "I said no," she panted. "And you *promised*."

He sat up abruptly, staring down at her with a stunned expression. He wasn't used to being told no, she could see.

He'd given her so much. Who was she to deny him his rights? She braced herself for his reaction.

Cameron blinked at the determined scrap of femininity before him. His breaths were deep and ragged as he worked to secure the remnants of his control.

His new bride had just put him very firmly in his place. Again.

He'd almost broken his promise, he thought ruefully. So cocksure—cock-ready!—he'd been that he could seduce her, that it was only nerves that had caused her ludicrous demand for a courtship. Who did their courting *after* the wedding?

But apparently she meant it. He glanced again at her pale, set face. Her slender body was stiff, and braced for . . . what? Did she expect him to explode in anger? Force her?

She did.

The realization shocked him. Did she know him so little?

The truth of that hit him hard—because of course she *didn't* know him, had no way of knowing that he'd never forced a woman in his life. Nor had he ever raised a hand in anger to any woman or child. Or ever would.

He wanted her more than any female he'd ever encountered. Her kisses and caresses had fired his blood like the strongest whisky. His body was rampant and aching, desire thick in his blood.

But she'd known him barely a day. And women were different. Women needed time.

She was his *wife*, not some girl up for a tumble in the grass. They had a lifetime to get to know each other. She'd come to him when she was ready, when he'd given her her blasted courtship. He would abide by his promise.

"Aye, you're right," he said quietly. "I didn't mean it to go so far. I'm sorry."

She didn't say anything, but watched him with big, doubtful blue eyes.

"Time for sleep." He pulled back the bedclothes to let her slide into them. He caught a glimpse of the spots of his blood, dark on the white sheet. Was she even a virgin at all? She hadn't kissed like a virgin.

Not that it mattered to him now. He was committed to her, publicly and privately.

She hesitated, then slipped past him and curled up on the far side of the big bed. She lay with her back to him, her bony little spine disappearing into her pretty nightdress. Her hair was pulled to one side, exposing her nape, pale, soft and vulnerable. He resisted the urge to kiss it. She was so small and delicate compared to him. But she was no weakling.

He liked that about her. Life with Jeannie would never be dull.

With a rueful smile Cameron slid in beside her. Reaching out, he pulled her towards him, tucking her securely against the curve of his body. She stiffened a moment, like a suspicious little twig.

"Only for sleep," he murmured, and slowly, achingly slowly, she relaxed against him.

Cameron lay in the dark, listening to the soft breathing of the woman in his arms. Twenty-four hours ago he'd had no thought of marrying, not until his argument with Uncle Charles. A wife then was a mere theoretical notion, to be considered at some time in the future.

Now he was a married man, with full control of his inheritance and the estate. He hadn't considered any but the legal implications, but now . . .

Now there was another person to be considered, in his life and in his bed. Perhaps the most important person in his life.

And he knew almost nothing about her.

Chapter Nine

BRIGHT SUNLIGHT PIERCED the gaps between the curtains. Jeannie stretched sleepily, then woke with a jerk as the events of the previous day—and night—flooded her awareness.

She was married. To the laird.

It could have been a dream—it was mad enough to be one—but the warmth and the comfort of the big bed were real enough.

At Grandad's she'd slept on a thin straw pallet on the floor, the covers heavy and scratchy, but never quite warm enough. And she was up every day before dawn, or Grandad would want to know the reason why.

Here, she lay on a soft, deep mattress, between fine cotton sheets. The blankets were thick and warm, woven from the softest wool. And judging by the light, it was well after sunrise. Yet nobody had come to wake her.

She turned her head cautiously. She was alone in the bed. She didn't remember him leaving, but she did recall drifting off to sleep with his big, hard body curved around her, warm against her back.

It had felt so strange . . . yet oddly right. She'd refused him. And he'd listened. And then he'd held her through the night, as if she were precious to him.

Surely that couldn't be right? She was simply a means to an end. Marriage for the sake of his inheritance. Any woman would have done. She'd been the lucky one, that was all.

She didn't want to get up to face the day. She would give anything to just snuggle down in the warmth, and pretend it really was all a dream, a delicious, fantastical dream.

But if there was one thing that Jeannie had learned in life, it was that nothing came free. This comfort, this warmth, the very position she'd been given—it all had to be earned.

She hadn't had much luck in her life, and she was grateful for the opportunity. She wouldn't waste it. Her husband might not be best pleased with her at the moment, but she'd make him a good wife, she was determined on it.

She ought to have asked him what he expected her to do today, but Cameron was gone, presumably off to do . . . whatever a laird did.

What did a laird's wife do? She considered the question.

He'd told her she'd be the woman of the house. He must have been laughing up his sleeve at that understatement. Still, that's where she'd start. She'd said yesterday that she'd inspect the household with that housekeeper woman, Mrs . . . Mrs. Findlay, that was it.

What then? Cameron's uncle seemed to be the cause of this hasty marriage. It might be as well to pay him a visit and see what she could learn. She did not want to be mistress of a warring house.

She was about to slide out of bed to wash and

dress and go in search of some breakfast, when a soft knock sounded at the door.

"Come in," Jeannie called.

Mairie, the maidservant, entered carrying a large jug of gently steaming water. "Good morning, m'lady, I hope you slept well. I've brought you hot water to wash in." She carefully set the jug on the washstand and turned with a self-conscious smile. "The Laird said you'd be sleeping late the morn, and to bring you your breakfast in bed. So, what would you like to eat?"

"What is there?" For the last six years, she'd eaten nothing but porridge for breakfast—and sometimes for dinner as well.

Mairie looked surprised. "Anything you want, m'lady. There's porridge, of course. And if you're still hungry there's eggs, any way you want, and black pudding, ham, kippers, toast—or bannock, if you prefer—whatever you like. And a pot of tea. Or chocolate, if that's your preference."

The choices dazzled her. "A boiled egg would be perfect, and a slice of toast. And tea. Is there any honey?"

"Of course, m'lady. Roskirk honey is the finest you'll ever taste," Mairie said proudly. She turned to leave, then looked back doubtfully. "So, no porridge at all?"

"No porridge," Jeannie said firmly. "Just a soft boiled egg and toast with honey."

Mairie left, and Jeannie slipped out of bed and padded barefoot across the room to make her ablutions. She slowed, frowning. The wooden floor felt slightly gritty underfoot. She peered down at it. The floor needed sweeping. And now she came to look more critically at her surroundings, she could see a faint layer of dust on the mantel. And the dressing table. And there was a cobweb in the corner of the ceiling.

Jeannie frowned. The room needed a good cleaning.

If she'd been an unexpected guest placed hastily in a little used bedchamber, there might have been an excuse for such slapdash housekeeping—though she didn't think so—but this was *the laird's bedchamber.* It should be gleaming with care at all times.

She remembered what she'd said to the housekeeper the previous night. *I can see for myself the castle is well run.*

She'd said it to be polite, that was all. She'd been too nervous yesterday to notice anything. But now, in the clear light of day, and with her wedding night behind her, she realized she'd spoken too soon.

Cameron, manlike, would probably not have noticed the faint air of neglect that was so obvious to her now. Last night the housekeeper had sent maids up to prepare the laird's bedchamber for his wedding night. Those sheets had been fresh and sweet smelling—Jeannie might have been nervous, but she'd noticed that. You could smell the sunshine in freshly washed and dried sheets.

So the maids had made up the bed with fresh sheets, but hadn't swept or mopped the floor or polished the furniture.

Jeannie couldn't imagine anyone neglecting such obvious tasks, especially when preparing the room for their laird on his wedding night. Cameron was obviously beloved by his people, so wouldn't they want his bedchamber to be perfect? Especially for such a night.

Could it be deliberate? An intentional slight? Or was it simply a matter of lazy or neglectful maids.

Thank God for Mam's experience as housekeeper in a great house.

She washed and dressed, pondering the day ahead of her. She expected some kind of hostility from Cameron's uncle—oh, he'd been all smooth politeness in front of an audience last night, but that would no doubt change once they were alone. She resolved to take tea with him this afternoon. Best to know from the start.

But first there was the house to inspect with the housekeeper, Mrs. Findlay. And the matter of a dusty bedchamber to be addressed.

She used Cameron's brush and arranged her hair in a loose knot. She stepped back and examined her reflection in the looking glass. And sighed. If only she had a different dress to wear, something smarter and a little bit more fashionable. Clothing was a kind of armor, and she was going into battle.

Legally she was the laird's wife—apart from the consummation—but she still had to earn her place.

"Mairie," Jeannie said when the girl returned with her breakfast on a tray. "The maids who prepared this room yesterday."

"Yes m'lady?" Mairie said cautiously.

"Have them come up, please"—she glanced at the clock on the overmantel—"in fifteen minutes."

Mairie left, and Jeannie turned to her breakfast. She surveyed the tray with pleasure. Her boiled egg sat in a blue flowered egg-cup, and beside it was a plate of golden toast, still warm, a small dish of butter and a pot of honey. A blue teapot was covered with a knitted cosy, and beside it sat a dainty cup and saucer with a matching jug containing milk. There was also a sprig of heather in a tiny vase.

The cook, at least, was taking pains to please the new mistress. The thought cheered her.

She cut the top off her egg and was pleased to see it was perfectly cooked: the white was firm and the yolk rich and runny. She dug in hungrily. It was the best breakfast she'd had in years. The only breakfast that wasn't porridge.

She was finishing her second cup of tea when Mairie returned with two worried-looking girls. She introduced them; Kirsty and Aileen. Kirsty was wringing her apron between nervous hands. The girls were close to Jeannie's own age, but their demeanor brought home to her how greatly her position had changed. She hoped they couldn't tell how nervous she was.

"You prepared this room yesterday, I gather," she said.

"Yes'm, but—"

"Tell me, was it your decision not to sweep the floor or dust the furniture?"

The girls exchanged glances. "I told you we should've—" Kirsty began, then bit her lip.

Aileen lifted her chin and said with an edge of defiance, "It was a busy day yesterday. There were more important things to do than to sweep a floor that Himself wouldna notice. Men don't."

"Did Mrs. Findlay tell you that?"

Aileen shrugged. "She inspected the room herself."

"I see. So this is how the women of Roskirk honor their laird? Leaving him with a dirty bedchamber—*on his wedding night*?" She spoke quietly, but Kirsty burst into tears.

"I'm sorry, ma'am. We honor the laird, truly we do. We didn't mean—" She looked at Aileen and broke off, sobbing into her handkerchief.

Aileen said nothing. She didn't look particularly repentant.

"I'll be speaking with Mrs. Findlay shortly," Jeannie said. "And some time after that I'll be taking tea with my husband's uncle. While I'm gone, I want this room swept, scrubbed and polished until it shines. When I return, I don't want to see a speck of dust or a single cobweb."

"Yes, m'lady," Kirsty said.

"If you've no other duties for me, m'lady, I'll help, too," Mairie said, and Jeannie nodded.

"And what if Mrs. Findlay wants us for something else?" Aileen asked. It was a clear challenge to Jeannie's authority.

She gave the girl a cool look. "I'll explain to Mrs. Findlay why you've been detained." She turned to leave and seeing the tumbled bedclothes, added, "Oh, and put fresh sheets on the bed, please." She tried not to blush.

"But it's no' washing day—" Kirsty began.

"Whisht, Kirsty," Mairie hissed, pulling a face in silent explanation. Kirsty looked puzzled at first, then turned bright red. Jeannie's face felt quite as hot.

There was nothing wrong in the maids thinking she'd gone a virgin to her marriage bed—that had been the point of Cameron's gallant gesture, after all— but she still felt guilty. And embarrassed.

She swept from the room, her cheeks aflame. Marriage in a castle was so very . . . public.

Chapter Ten

CAMERON STRADDLED THE ridge board of the roof as he hammered down battens. The rafters were already in—they were making good progress. The roof belonged to the cottage of Bridget Fraser, a young widow with three wee bairns. Bridget's man had been killed in an accident the previous spring.

Cameron had sent his cousins off to clear away the debris of the wrecked bridge, and had organized several other, more skilled men to work with him. Bridget's roof was the worst damaged by the big storm. And having originally been made generations before with bits and bobs of driftwood, it had shattered under the onslaught of the storm and now needed a whole new framework as well as new thatch.

"Thank you so much for this, Laird," Bridget said when he arrived. "My father-in-law has sheltered us since the storm, but it's no' a big cottage and with three lively bairns underfoot, well"—she grimaced—"he's a good man, but no' the most patient of beings."

Cameron laughed. Bridget's father-in-law was famously irascible. It was one of the things he'd taken into account in deciding whose roof would be repaired first.

He hammered briskly, enjoying the activity and the thin morning sunshine, and glad to be able to make the repairs that had gnawed at him while his uncle was in control.

And Bridget had called him Laird. It was still a new enough appellation to make him smile. He was laird at last, with a wife and all.

A wife. In name only at this stage. She wanted courting first. Courting! And poetry! He wasn't the kind of man who spouted poetry. He glanced at Robbie Ross, busily laying thatch at the other end of the roof.

"Robbie, when you were courting Jessie, what kind of things did you do?"

Robbie snorted. "No' enough, I can tell you. Jessie's da' kept his eye on us the whole time. And if it wasn't her da' with us, it was her ma, or her granny."

Cameron grinned. "Aye, but apart from no' doing what you itched to do, what did Jessie like about the courting?

Robbie didn't look up from his thatching. "Och, she liked me to bring her little gifts. I gave her a hair comb once that pleased her well, things like that. Mostly we sat with the old folks looking on, trying to think of things to talk about. But usually after a few minutes her da' would find me some wee job to do around the place, and after that Jessie or her mam would make me a cup of tea and that was it—off home for me. A quick kiss if I was lucky, and most of the time I wasn't."

Robbie sat back, viewed his progress and reached for another bundle of thatch. He glanced at Cameron and added, "You made the right choice, man—skippin' the courtship and going straight to marriage."

Cameron gave him a half-smile. He hadn't skipped anything, he'd just done it the other way around.

Bridget brought them mugs of tea a short time later. She must have overheard their conversation, for she said in a quiet voice, "My John and I used to take long walks when we were courting, along the beach, by the woods. Mostly we just talked. And listened. By the time we were wed, we knew each other so well there was no question of bridal nerves for me."

Cameron tried not to notice the unshed tears glistening in her eyes. "John wasn't much of a talker, as I recall."

She smiled. "You learn about a person as much by what they don't say, as what they say. More sometimes. And also by what they do. She glanced up at Robbie Ross drinking his tea on the roof, and added softly, "Nobody ever had to ask my John to do anything. He saw something that needed to be done, and did it. Quietly, without fuss or fanfare."

Cameron nodded. "Aye, he was a fine man, your John."

She swallowed. "He was. This roof would have been fixed long since if he hadn't been . . . " She looked away and after a moment said in a choked voice, "My thanks to you, Laird."

Cameron nodded. He put down his empty cup and climbed back up onto the roof with a renewed sense of purpose. This was why he'd married Jeannie McLeay—to do for people like Bridget what they could not do for themselves.

What he hadn't taken into account was how he would feel about his new bride.

The way Jeannie had looked when he left her this morning, curled up in the bed, all soft and warm, her hair spread across the pillow. It had taken all of his willpower to simply slide out of bed and pad quietly away. Leaving her serenely sleeping. Untouched.

He hammered down another strut. Unspoken in what Bridget had said was a clear sense that she and her John had enjoyed each other. In all ways. Especially in bed.

The sooner this blasted courtship of his was done with the better.

He thought about Robbie's wife, and how her watchful, protective family made sure that Robbie treated her right before the wedding. Jeannie had no-one to look after her interests, only that useless grandfather, who took better care of his sheep than his granddaughter.

And yet his Jeannie had stood up for herself. Not many brides would have the courage to deny a laird his marital rights and further, to demand a courtship. That took courage.

He liked that in her. A laird's wife needed courage.

Talking and listening and walks. He could do that. And little gifts. Anything, as long as he didn't have to spout poetry.

Jeannie's tour of the castle was enlightening—but also a little puzzling. The housekeeper, Mrs. Findlay, seemed to be as efficient as she looked. She answered all of Jeannie's questions crisply and in detail and, on the surface at least, Jeannie couldn't fault her organization. Or her attitude, though she was a little intimidating.

Yet in quite a number of rooms there was a faint but definite air of neglect—furniture that was dusty, cobwebs in a few places, carpets that needed a good beating. The dust showed all the more because Roskirk Castle was such a bare and barren-looking place. It wasn't filthy, Jeannie thought. But it wasn't spotless, and it ought to be.

She decided to broach the matter with the housekeeper. "This morning I sent for the maids who were supposed to clean the laird's bedchamber. Kirsty and Aileen."

The tall housekeeper frowned. "Supposed to? They did clean it, I checked."

"Well, be that as it may, it wasn't cleaned to my satisfaction. I've asked them to clean it again."

Jeannie half expected Mrs. Findlay to argue, or give some excuse, but though her frown deepened, she didn't respond to the criticism in any way. She didn't even seem offended, just thoughtful. She continued the tour, but seemed a little abstracted.

The only part of the castle Jeannie could find no fault with was in the area ruled by the cook—the kitchens and scullery. Everything was immaculate, from the well-scrubbed stone flags to the gleaming pots and pans hanging on the wall. Mrs. Baird, the cook, had greeted Jeannie with friendly courtesy and cheerfully gave her a tour, ending with her suggestions for meals for the next few days. Jeannie approved them all.

Mrs. Findlay stood back, playing no part in the conversation, waiting in silence. Clearly the two women ruled separate domains, but Jeannie could detect no apparent animosity between them.

As they walked down the passage leading away from the kitchen, they passed a door. "Where does that lead?" Jeannie asked.

"The kitchen garden." Mrs. Findlay kept walking.

"I'd like to see it."

"There's not much growing at this season, but if you wish . . . " The housekeeper opened the door and led the way into a large high-walled garden. It was neatly arranged in beds, with narrow cinder pathways winding through it. Fruit trees had been espaliered against the south wall and there was a substantial greenhouse in the corner. Jeannie was delighted.

"Can we see inside the greenhouse, please?"

With a faint, acquiescent shrug, Mrs. Findlay led the way. They turned a corner around some gooseberry bushes and Jeannie came to an abrupt halt. Stretched across the pathway a large cobweb hung, the strands glistening faintly in the sun. Mrs. Findlay didn't slacken her pace.

Clearly she had no fear of spiders. Jeannie hung back, waiting for her to deal with it. But to her horror, the housekeeper walked straight into the web—and recoiled with a loud exclamation and frantic gestures.

Jeannie rushed forward and helped her brush the sticky strands off her face and hair, assuring her that there was no spider on her. "I saw you walking toward it, but I thought you were going to knock it down with a stick or something," she said.

"No, I didn't— " The woman bit her tongue and looked away.

And suddenly Jeannie understood. "You didn't see it, did you?"

Mrs. Findlay said nothing.

"Your eyesight is going, isn't it?" Jeannie said softly. Of course. That was why the maids had been able to get away with slapdash work.

There was a short silence. "What makes you say that?"

"I've been wondering why, when you're such an efficient and well-organized person, the castle is in need of a good clean."

"A good clean?" Mrs. Findlay repeated stiffly.

"You can't see it, but there is a faint layer of dust on much of the furniture, and even some cobwebs in some rooms."

Mrs. Findlay sagged. "I suppose it's no use pretending any longer. The last year or so it's been getting worse. I've tried spectacles, but they do nae good. I can barely even read my own writing." She straightened and said with dignity, "You'll be wanting to dismiss me, then."

Jeannie thought for a minute. "I don't think that will be necessary."

Mrs. Findlay looked at her with a shocked expression. "But you said the castle was *dirty!* You cannot want—" She swallowed and said with quiet dignity. "I have always prided myself on the quality of my work. If I can no longer perform to the required standard—"

"As I said, your organization seems first rate to me. It is just your eyesight that is letting you down."

"Just my eyesight," Mrs. Findlay echoed bitterly. "The most important part. If I canna see whether the girls have done a good job—"

"No, but I can."

There was a short silence, then Jeannie said, "If you will continue to organize the castle, I will be your eyes—for the moment, at least—and I'll try to be discreet about it." Though it was clear the maids knew. "Have you had your eyes examined by a specialist?"

Mrs. Findlay snorted. "I don't need some doctor to tell me I'm going blind. I can see that for myself." She sighed and added in a defeated voice. "My mother's eyesight went the same way—she was blind before she was sixty."

"Well, we'll cross that bridge when we come to it," Jeannie said. "Now, let us inspect the greenhouse."

Mrs. Findlay didn't move. "You'll have to tell the laird. I canna go on deceiving him."

"I'll tell him, but he did promise me that the household was mine to run, so there's no need to worry." Cameron might have thought it a grand joke when he'd told her she'd be 'the woman of the house' but she intended to hold him to it.

Mrs. Findlay still didn't move. Her eyes filled with tears. "Are you sure about this, lass?"

"Very sure," Jeannie assured her gently. She knew what it was like to be alone and dependent on the good will of others. Besides, this woman was almost fearsomely efficient, apart from her eyesight. "Now then, let's look at that greenhouse. I'll be having tea with my husband's uncle this afternoon, and I'll need to wash and tidy myself first. He seems to me to be a very elegant gentleman. And possibly hard to please? My marriage won't exactly have endeared me to him." She ended on a questioning note, hoping the housekeeper might give her a hint or two about Charles Sinclair.

His extreme old-fashioned elegance and courtly manners were a little overwhelming, especially for a girl who everyone knew had been fished out of a bog. And was still wearing the same blue dress she'd been married in.

Worse still, her marriage had stripped him of all power and influence.

Mrs. Findlay opened the greenhouse door. "Och, Mr. Charles is no' so bad. He's bored, that's all. And mebbe a bit lonely. He's no' an outdoors sort of gentleman, so he gets no pleasure from hunting or fishing like the other men do. He's all for society and art and things like that—he paints, you know, and plays music on his spinet. He was reared in the French court."

"Ah." That made sense.

They finished the tour of the greenhouse and the kitchen garden. At the base of the stairs, Jeannie paused when Mrs. Findlay laid a hand on her arm. "You truly mean it about being my eyes, m'lady? You'll not dismiss me?"

"Of course not," Jeannie said softly "I think we'll make a good team, don't you?" The older woman nodded, wordlessly.

Jeannie hurried upstairs. To her delight, the bed-chamber was now spotless, with every surface burnished and fragrant with the scent of beeswax polish. The carpets, now well beaten, glowed with color and the floor had been mopped and polished to a soft sheen. Even the window panes were freshly washed and gleamed, crystal clear.

She turned slowly, noting every change for the better, and smiled. Not a speck of dust or shred of cobweb anywhere. It was a tiny victory. Her first step in becoming the wife of the laird. Next, to get the whole castle looking like this.

She washed her face and hands, and tidied her hair, then grimaced at her reflection, wishing she had another dress to change into.

On that thought, she sent for Mairie. "Is there a seamstress in the village, Mairie?"

Mairie gave her a doubtful look. "Why do you want to know?"

Jeannie gestured at her dress. "I can't go on in the same dress every day, can I?"

Mairie shook her head. "Most of the women in the village make their own dresses, but"—she hurried on before Jeannie could interrupt—"they're simple, hard-wearing garments, m'lady. No' at all all suitable for you. No' for the laird's lady."

"Having one dress to my name is just as unsuitable," Jeannie said briskly. "So I have no choice. Ask around for me, will you, Mairie, and see if you can find someone willing and capable."

"Aye m'lady." She didn't look at all happy.

Jeannie's next hurdle was tea with Cameron's uncle, the man he'd ousted by marrying her.

She wasn't looking forward to it.

Chapter Eleven

CAMERON SAT BACK on the roof beam and looked about him with some satisfaction. His work here was done; the rest was up to the thatchers. Two houses over, another roof was being repaired, and the village was busy with purposeful activity. His marriage, and his consequent ability to take control as the laird, had given the place new life. New hope.

He sent a lad to fetch his horse. Next he would ride out to the site of the ruined bridge and see how his cousins were getting on.

He'd sent them out first thing in the morning, with orders to clear away the wreckage and sort it into wood that could still be used, and firewood. He had long ago compiled a list of the necessary supplies, and had sent them off by sea the first night of his marriage, while he was waiting for her to be ready for him.

How was his bride getting on? If the repairs needed hadn't been so urgent, he might have stayed and broken his fast with her, discussed possibilities for the day, and eased her more gently into her new life.

But the state of some of the ruined roofs and the wrecked bridge—and the imminence of winter—

were the very reasons he'd married her in the first place.

He hoped she was managing. He'd begin his courtship this very evening, and take her for a walk by the sea. And talk, though about what he had no idea.

"You're off then, Laird?" Bridget said as he stepped off the ladder.

"Aye, out to the ruined bridge." A brisk breeze had sprung up, though there was, luckily, no sign of rain.

"Once we move back into the cottage I'll be able to get back to my weaving. There's scant room for it in my father-in-law's."

"Weaving?" Cameron echoed vaguely. He'd been thinking about the bridge. There was no time to build a stone bridge, not before winter, but next summer he promised himself he'd make a start on it. In the meantime, a wooden bridge would allow a resumption of contact with the outside world.

"Aye, Laird, and these days it's no' simply a pastime. The money I earn makes a real difference."

With an effort, Cameron recalled she'd been talking about her weaving. "You sell it?"

Bridget nodded. "There's a shop down in Edinburgh that buys my pieces—mine and some of the other women's. It seems city folk have lost the art of weaving. The man in Edinburgh sends us the money when each piece is sold. It's no' a lot, but it makes a difference, especially with three growing bairns."

"That's grand," he murmured. He was anxious to get on out to the bridge.

"Would you like to see some of my work, Laird? It's but a short step to my father-in-law's house." She was clearly proud of her weaving, and Cameron hesitated but a moment before he nodded. As laird, it behooved him to show an interest.

"I use the finest lambswool I can get," Bridget explained as they walked. "And sometimes, if I get a rabbit or two, I spin in some of the fur. It's very soft and adds a lovely texture. And of course, I spin and dye and weave it all myself."

She laid several of her shawls out on the table at her father-in-law's cottage. The old man sat by, smoking his pipe, watching with a dour expression. The two older children had been playing knucklebones in the corner, while the baby gnawed on a crust. They'd all fallen silent when Cameron entered.

Cameron had never taken much notice of what women wore—not shawls, anyway—but he could see why the shop in Edinburgh bought Bridget's weavings. They were so soft and fine, not like home-spun at all, and the colors glowed like jewels against the drab setting of the cottage.

His fingers hovered over a soft shawl in a deep, rich blue with a hint of lavender. "How much would you sell this for?"

"To the man in Edinburgh?" He nodded, and she named a price he thought shockingly small.

"And how much does he sell them for in his shop?"

"I'm not exactly sure, but some one told me a friend in Edinburgh had seen one of my shawls for"—she named a price—"but that couldn't be right. It's far too expensive."

Cameron frowned. He'd have to investigate this Edinburgh fellow. He wasn't going to allow his people to be cheated, and it sounded as though that might be the case. But when would he have time to go to Edinburgh? Maybe he'd take Jeannie on a belated bride trip.

"Would you sell me that one?" He pointed to the blue shawl.

Bridget looked shocked. "Sell it, Laird? After you've worked all day on my cottage roof? I should think not! I'll give it gladly."

"Then I'll not take it." He glanced at her father-in-law, then back at Bridget and said firmly, "I'm the laird now, Bridget. I'm well aware of the neglect that's taken place since Uncle Ian died and I'm going to be working on every ruined roof that needs it—no special favors. Now, I want to buy this shawl as a gift for my bride, but I'll not be cheating you or any one of my tenants out of what they're due. So will you sell it to me or not?"

"Och, but it's not my finest shawl—there's a wee imperfection in the corner, see?" She pointed but Cameron could see nothing amiss.

"It's fine."

"The pink one is daintier, or how about this white one? White is very suitable for a bride." But his hand rested possessively on the blue shawl, and seeing it, she smiled. "Very well. I can see you want the blue one."

"I do." He laid a sum of money on the table and she gasped.

"But that's far too much!"

It was exactly what she'd said the shop in Edinburgh sold them for. He raised his brow. "Are you saying I'm no' as good as the fancy folk in Edinburgh?"

She gave an awkward half-laugh. "Of course not."

"Then we'll not be arguing." He folded the pretty blue shawl up and tucked it under his arm.

Bridget, her father-in-law and the little ones followed him to the door of the cottage. "Thank you,

Laird," Bridget said. "For everything. My very best wishes to your bride."

The lad was waiting outside with his horse. Cameron tucked the shawl into his saddlebag. His first courting gift. He'd give it to her this evening.

He mounted his horse and rode away toward the causeway and the ruined bridge where he'd first met a feisty scrap, all mud and wary suspicion, with a pair of blazing blue eyes that had pierced him to the heart. And his whole life had changed.

He thought about the way she'd kissed him the previous night, the softness of her lips and wild honey taste of her. The way her slender limbs had twined around him.

Lord, but he wanted her something fierce.

He wished he could have spent more time with her this morning, given her a proper honeymoon. But these repairs were urgent and while the good weather held, he could not give his bride the attention she deserved.

He hoped she liked the shawl.

———

Jeannie took a deep breath, smoothed her hair and her skirts for the dozent time, and knocked on Charles Sinclair's door.

"*Entrez!*" She hoped he didn't intend to conduct the whole conversation in French. She spoke a little French but wasn't very fluent.

A slight, dark-haired manservant opened the door and stepped back with a welcoming gesture. The tall figure of Cameron's uncle rose to greet her.

"Good morning, Mr. Sinclair, I . . ." Her voice trailed off as she looked around her in amazement.

It was as if by stepping through the door she'd been transported from a Scottish castle of plain gray stone and wood to . . . to some sumptuous French palace. It was all lightness and gold and richly textured color.

The bedchamber she shared with her husband was lined with dark wooden paneling. Here the same kind of paneling had been painted white, and was ornamented with elegant gold-leafed molding. The stone walls above the paneling had been plastered and covered with delicately embossed pale green paper.

The floorboards, too, were painted white, and scattered with thick Persian rugs, richly colored and soft underfoot. On either side of a tall, white enamel stove hung huge, ornately gold-framed paintings of an aristocratic-looking man and a beautiful woman, both wearing high white wigs and sumptuous clothing. Echoes of a past age of elegance.

"My parents," Charles Sinclair murmured.

Crimson velvet curtains framed the windows. On the opposite wall another window framed a scene of bucolic delight, hills and trees and a pretty shepherdess in an old-fashioned dress trimmed with lace—lace? On a shepherdess? She was watching over sheep that looked like small fluffy clouds against the lush, green grass. Cleaner than any sheep Jeannie had ever seen.

She frowned, looking at those sheep. She moved closer and looked again. She glanced at the windows on the opposite wall. They looked out on a grey Scottish day in late autumn, all soft muted colors; slate gray, lilac, grey-green. She looked again at the shepherdess standing in bright sunshine in a colorful flower-dotted meadow. It didn't make sense. Apart from the very unScottish scene, this window was facing the wrong way—inward.

"*Trompe l'oeil*," Charles Sinclair said. "Do you like it? I painted it myself."

"You *painted* this?" Jeannie moved closer, and saw that it was indeed a painting. "But it looks so real. I'd heard you painted, but I had no idea . . ."

She examined the tiny figures, the illusion of lace on the shepherdess's dress, small exquisite details such as the tiny flowers growing in the grass and a bird pulling a worm from the earth. Everything looked so real until you were a few inches away from it and saw the texture of the paint.

"It's wonderful. I've never seen anything like it." Things that close up seemed like random blobs and smears, when you stepped a few feet away they turned into lifelike images.

"It's an old technique," Charles Sinclair said carelessly, though it was clear he was delighted by her praise. "Been around since the Romans."

"You're very talented." Jeannie glanced around the suite of rooms. "And these rooms are extraordinary—so different from any other part of the castle."

He gave a very French shrug that managed to combine modesty with smugness. "One craves some semblance of civilization in these grim gray surrounds. If one cannot be in Versailles . . . " He pouted. "I would have transformed the whole castle thusly, had my nephew not rushed off so intemperately and—" He broke off, remembering who he was talking to. "But where are my manners? Please be seated. Gustave, tea for madame." He snapped his fingers and his manservant brought forward a silver tray bearing a dainty tea service, and a plate of pretty cakes and biscuits.

Jeannie seated herself on a spindly, gilt-trimmed,

crimson-cushioned chair and received her cup from the manservant.

Charles Sinclair sipped his tea. "I had planned to enliven that big barren hall with silk hangings from Paris, made to my own design, but it is not to be. My nephew cancelled the order and that was that."

"Yes, he mentioned the hangings," Jeannie murmured.

He sniffed. "I suppose he was gloating."

"Not at all. But he intimated that money was scarce and he had more urgent matters to attend to," she said diplomatically.

Charles Sinclair sniffed again. "Roofs. For peasants."

She sipped her tea and said nothing. She agreed with her husband's priorities, but there was no point in arguing.

"My hangings would have made all the difference in the world to that great gloomy barn downstairs." He put his teacup down. "Would you care to see my designs for them?" He didn't wait for her response, but snapped his fingers at Gustave and rapped out an order in French.

A moment later the manservant brought out a folio and laid it out for Jeannie to view. Charles Sinclair leaned forward. "Well? What do you think?"

"They're very elegant and very beautiful," she said. "Very French."

He sat back, pleased with her response.

It wasn't flattery. The designs were beautiful. But the hangings would have looked quite out of place in the hall, she decided, a bit like a bird of paradise in a flock of grouse. They were dainty and pretty. The hall was a little grim, but it was also magnificent.

It called for something more dramatic and . . . and *Scottish*. But she didn't say so.

She'd dreaded this meeting with her husband's uncle, and had come braced for hostility. Instead she'd found a man very much out of his element, a lonely, cultured man who felt unappreciated. She nibbled on a cake and tried to think of something to say.

"You have an eye for art," he said. "I admit to some surprise, given your background."

She stifled a sigh. No doubt she'd always be described as the shepherdess bride who was hauled from a bog. "I don't know much about it, but my father had several friends who were artists."

He raised a brow. "Your father, was he an artist too?"

"No, he was a poet."

He frowned. "His name?"

"Alexander McLeay."

He gave her an arrested look, then snapped his fingers at his manservant. "The slender blue volume on the third shelf."

Gustave fetched the book and made to hand it to his master, who waved him away. "To the lady, *imbécile*."

Jeannie took the little book, a pretty thing bound in blue leather. She opened it. "Oh! It's Da's book! Imagine you having it." She examined it carefully, marveling at seeing it here, of all places.

She glanced up at Charles Sinclair watching her. "You must think I'm a little odd, but the thing is I've never seen the properly bound version. Da couldn't afford to have many done, and they all went to be sold. My only copy was bound with a simple card-board cover." Handmade by Mam.

"Indeed?"

She nodded. "Mam and Da quarreled over this binding. Mam said we couldn't afford leather—poets don't make very much money, you see. But Da not only ignored her, he chose the blue leather, which was the most expensive. Mam was so cross with him—at first."

The elderly man raised a brow. "At first?"

"Yes. Da's explanation to my mother was, 'Of course it had to be blue. Blue to match my beloved's eyes.' Naturally Mam couldn't stay cross with him after that." She gave a misty smile, remembering. "Da was a romantic."

"Of course he was," Charles Sinclair declared. "He was an artist, a poet." There was a short silence, then he added, "You said your only copy was cardboard. *Was?*"

She nodded. "It was . . . destroyed." Grandad had lost his temper with her one day and had hurled it into the fire.

"Then you must keep this copy."

"Oh, but I couldn't—"

"No, no. I insist. Call it a bride gift."

She swallowed, deeply touched by his unexpected generosity. "Thank you, Mr. Sinclair. It's very kind of you. I will treasure it always, and not only because of my father."

He gave her an approving little nod. "Against all expectations, my nephew seems to have chosen well. Welcome to the family, my dear. I am delighted to be related by marriage to the daughter of Alexander McLeay. You must call me Uncle Charles."

He gave her a long considering look and added imperiously, "I will paint your portrait. I doubt my nephew will appreciate it—he cares only for such things as roofs and the needs of peasants—but you will admire it, I know, sensitive poet's daughter that you are."

Jeannie thanked him again. She didn't consider herself to be particularly sensitive—she'd had to be quite tough to survive life with Grandad—but she was grateful for the approval and acceptance of this gentle, eccentric old man.

"Thank you for coming to take tea with me, my dear. Come and visit me any time. Now I find myself fatigued." He leaned back in his chair, closed his eyes, and to all appearances went instantly to sleep. His manservant edged forward, silently indicating to Jeannie that the interview was over.

Amused and a little bemused, she rose and tiptoed out, clutching the precious blue book to her bosom. The interview she'd dreaded had resulted in an entirely unexpected outcome. Instead of resentment and enmity she'd been given a warm welcome and a precious memento. Da's book. Imagine that.

Chapter Twelve

MAIRIE MUST HAVE mentioned Jeannie's request for a seamstress to Mrs. Findlay, for shortly after she'd left Charles Sinclair's rooms, the housekeeper approached her. "Homespun is not at all suitable for the laird's lady," she said bluntly. "But we might find something we can use in the attic."

Jeannie spent the next hour in the attic with Mairie and Mrs. Findlay, going through the old dresses left by Cameron's mother, searching for suitable fabric to reuse.

Jeannie sat back on her heels, dismayed. "It's all very fine, but . . . " They'd gone through three large trunks and a number of smaller boxes. A wealth of old clothing, almost none of it usable.

The shoes were impossible. Cameron's mother had tiny feet.

They'd found plenty of dresses and other garments, including a fine tartan shawl that Jeannie shook out and draped around herself. It was moth-eaten in one corner, but she could hide that in the folds, she thought.

There were some fine linen petticoats that they decided could be made into underclothes. But none of the other fabrics were suitable for the kind of everyday dresses Jeannie was in need of.

Cameron's mother's gowns were all from another time, made of stiff brocades or heavily embroidered silks, satin, damask, and velvet. Jeannie put aside several to be made into dresses for wearing to church, and for when they might have visitors to entertain, though both Mairie and Mrs. Findlay seemed to think a village seamstress might not be up to working with such fabrics.

The local women were, they reminded her, more used to wool. And very plain styles at that.

"These won't do at all," Mrs. Findlay declared, replacing the old dresses in their yellowed tissue wrapping and shutting the trunk lid firmly. "The laird must take you down to Inverness, or better still, Edinburgh, where the fashionable dressmakers are to be found. His mother, after all, had everything of the best, and from Paris."

Like her brother, Charles, Jeannie thought. But she was no fancy French born aristocrat to be demanding the finest of everything. Cameron had been worried enough about his uncle's spending. Far be it for her to add to those worries.

As for a trip to Inverness or Edinburgh, Jeannie couldn't see that happening any time soon. Cameron was wholly concerned with estate matters. It would be petty of her to demand a shopping trip to Edinburgh, when he was racing against time to ensure his people were snug and secure and well sheltered from the winter cold.

"Homespun will suffice for the time being," Jeannie decided. "And some shoes from the village shoemaker." Anything was better than wearing the same dress day after day, and too-big shoes stuffed with wool.

Mrs. Findlay sniffed, but said nothing.

❧

Cameron arrived home late that afternoon, tired, dusty and itching from bits of thatching straw caught in his hair and clothing, but well pleased. They'd made a good start on the repairs that the estate so badly needed.

Not wanting to present himself to his wife in his dusty state, he'd stripped to his breeks and washed under the pump in the yard behind the kitchen.

Clean, refreshed and still dripping, he stepped inside. "Afternoon Mrs. Baines. Something smells good. Would you happen to know where I might find my wife?"

The cook shook her head. „Laird, Laird, Laird. Must ye drip water all over my good clean floor?" She handed him a towel

Cameron grinned and dutifully towel-dried his dripping torso and hair. Having known Mrs. Baines all his life, he appreciated the slightly acerbic undertone she'd given to "Laird," giving him to understand that as far as she was concerned he was still the grubby urchin who'd tracked mud across her floors, stealing biscuits and cakes on the way. He tossed her the damp towel and eyed a batch of oatcakes, fresh from the oven and cooling on a rack.

She followed his gaze. "Don't you dare—och! Serve you right if you burn your mouth."

He demolished the hot oatcake in two bites. "My wife?"

"Upstairs, I think. She took tea this afternoon with your uncle. Last I heard she was in her bedchamber. Mrs. Findlay might know."

Cameron frowned. Damn his uncle. What the devil had he said to Jeannie? He knew he shouldn't have left her alone on this first day. He should have gone with her to Uncle Charles, defended her from his snobbery and superior attitudes. Grabbing another oatcake, he hurried away and took the stairs two at a time.

Quietly he opened his bedchamber door and found Jeannie curled up in the window seat, reading a small blue book. "Jeannie?"

She looked up and to his acute dismay, her eyes were filled with tears. It was worse than a punch in the chest

The bastard. He crossed the floor in two strides. "What did he say to you—och, don't look at me like that, lass—I'll send him away." He pulled out a handkerchief, saw it was dirty, tossed it aside and used his thumbs to gently wipe her tears away. Her skin was like silk. "Tell me what he said."

She blinked. "What who said?"

"My cursed uncle. Whatever he's done, I'll fix it."

Her brow puckered slightly. "But he was very kind."

"*Kind?*"

She nodded and held up the book. "He gave me this."

Cameron glanced at the book. "A book?"

She gave a shaky little laugh, tears and smiles at the same time. "Not just any book." She opened it and showed him the title page. "My very favorite book in all the world."

Cameron stared at it glumly as she burbled happily on. Poetry, he might have known.

"And then, when he found out I didn't own a copy, he gave me his. As a bride gift." Tears welled again, but her smile was luminous. "I've been reading and rereading it all afternoon."

"Ah. A bride gift." And one that from her reaction would be a thousand times better than his own simple blue shawl. Poetry. Cameron stared at her helplessly, then bent and carefully thumbed her tears away.

Her eyes dropped to his chest. And stayed there.

Cameron abruptly recalled that he was naked from the waist up. His mouth dried.

A single tear remained, glistening on her cheek. It took all his strength not to kiss it from her, to taste the salt of her tears and the fragrance of her skin.

She seemed absorbed by his chest, his very bare chest. It was a slow caress, almost tangible, though she hadn't moved a muscle. He swallowed.

Her gaze dropped to where skin met breeks.

His stomach muscles clenched with the effort to fight his growing arousal.

She wasn't trying to seduce him, he could tell. He'd been seduced by enough girls and women to know the difference between calculated seductiveness, and feminine curiosity.

The temptation to lean forward and encourage that curiosity was overwhelming. But he knew what would follow—his body was one great aching knot of lust for her—and his control was on a knife edge.

But he'd promised her a courtship before any bedding. A fortnight to wait, dammit.

Her gaze dropped briefly below the belt-line, then skittered away. Blushing, she moistened her lips.

Cameron groaned and leaned forward to capture them. His mouth had barely touched hers when there was a knock on the door and a voice called, "Laird, are you in there?"

Cameron groaned, a very different groan this time, and rose to his feet, cursing under his breath. He strode across the room and pulled open the door. "Yes?"

A servant stood there holding out a blue bundle. "Cook said you left this beside the pump when you had your wash."

Cameron tucked the shawl under his arm. "Anything else?"

"No, Laird."

"Tell Cook—oh, never mind." He closed the door, and turned to find her standing in front of the window, gazing out as if transfixed by the view. But she was breathing fast, as if she'd been running. And though he could only see her profile, her color was heightened.

He smiled to himself and pulled a clean shirt from the chest of drawers. The interruption was probably for the best. He'd come home early in order to get some courting done.

He pulled on the shirt and as he tucked it in, he glanced around the room, wondering how to broach the subject. Perplexed he wrinkled his brow. The room looked the same, only . . . it wasn't. And now he came to think of it, there was a distinct smell of beeswax.

"What have you done to this room?"

She jumped and turned around. "Nothing. I only had it cleaned. Properly." She sounded defensive.

He gave the room another swift examination. "Looks good. Smells good, too."

She smiled and gave a brisk little nod. "So much for men not noticing."

"Not noticing what?"

"Whether a room is clean or dirty."

He frowned. "Who said we didn't?"

"It doesn't matter. What was it that Cook sent up?"

"Oh, nothing much." He was only too aware that his gift was paltry compared with his uncle's. "I thought you might like to go for a walk by the sea tonight, before we dine."

"I would, thank you. But what has that to do with—oh." She broke off as he handed her a bundle.

"I got you this. Thought you might need something. The breeze off the sea can be quite chilly." And where, he wondered, were the gracious manners his uncle—both his uncles—had tried to drum into him? And the charm with which he'd been able to approach women in the past.

Small and unassuming though she was, something in her quiet composure—or was it the look in those wide blue eyes?—whatever, it brought out the great awkward lummox in him.

She shook out the shawl. "Oh, Cameron, it's beautiful." She wrapped it around her shoulders and turned to look at her reflection in the looking glass.

Cameron gave a satisfied nod. "I thought so. It matches perfectly."

"Matches?" She turned and gave him a puzzled look. "But it's quite a different blue from that of my dress—not that I mind, of course, but—"

Placing his hands on her shoulders, he turned her to face the looking glass again. "Not your dress, your eyes. Bridget was trying to push a pink shawl on me, or white for a bride, but I wanted this one because I knew it would match your bonny blue eyes. And it does. Perfectly."

Their eyes met in the looking glass, and under his appalled gaze, her eyes slowly filled with tears.

Not again. Cameron was frantic to stop them. "What is it? Do you not like it? Don't worry, I'll get rid of it, get you another." He went to peel the shawl from her shoulders.

Her hands closed over his. "Don't you dare."

"But—"

"I love it, Cameron. It's so soft and beautiful and warm. But most of all, I love that you chose it to match my eyes."

"But you're crying."

She gave that husky little laugh, half laughter, half tears, that caught him by the throat every time. "Yes, but they're happy tears."

Happy tears? He stood staring over her shoulder at her reflection in the looking glass. He was drowning, all at sea, anchored only by the warmth of her body leaning lightly against him and her small, strong hands resting on his. And the look in those blue, blue eyes, shining with tears.

Happy tears.

Once upon a time—a couple of days ago—he'd imagined he understood women just fine. The truth was, he hadn't a clue.

Chapter Thirteen

CAMERON LED JEANNIE down a narrow
pathway that wound away from the castle,
down toward the sea. They were climbing a slight
hill when Jeannie suddenly stopped dead. She closed
her eyes and drew several deep breaths.

"Are you all r—"

"Oh, how I've missed that smell." She threw back
her head and drew in another deep, luxuriant breath.
"Isn't it glorious? So clean and sharp and salty. It
does a body good just to breathe it in."

She dropped his arm and hurried up the last rise
to where the sea lay spread out before them. She
wrapped her arms around herself, pulling the blue
shawl tight as she stood staring out to sea, gazing
hungrily at the endless horizon.

He came up behind her, and without taking her
gaze from the shifting gray-blue waters and the
endless frills of white foam breaking on the shore,
she put her hand out for him. He took it, and she
squeezed his hand hard.

"Thank you for bringing me here. I'd . . . I'd
forgotten how much I'd missed this. I hadn't
realized . . . "

He watched her in fascination. "You're not sad to leave the hills?"

She shook her head. "The hills are bonny, and I do love the mist in the mountains, and the scent of heather, but I was born on an island. I grew up with the sound and scent of the sea all around me. I missed it something fierce when I was sent to live up in the hills with Grandad."

She drew another breath deep into her lungs, then gave him a mischievous look. "Race you to the water!" She darted, fleet-foot and nimble down the path and across the rocks toward the narrow, sandy beach.

With a shout of laughter, Cameron followed. His heavy boots slowed him down, but his legs were longer and he slowly gained on her.

She hit the beach and with barely a pause, kicked off her shoes, dropped the shawl on the clean, dry sand and sped on, her feet sending up tiny spurts of sand as she raced toward the water.

She didn't stop when she reached the water, just hitched up her skirts and danced into the sea as if in her natural element. Knee-deep in the shallows with her skirts bunched around her thighs, the waves foaming around her long, slender legs, she watched him with a provocative expression.

Lord, but she had a pair of legs on her. Doing his best to block the image of them wrapped around his waist, he waded into the water after her.

"You'll ruin your boots."

Cameron didn't care about his boots. He was all fired up. He closed in on her.

She splashed him and danced back, laughing. The water swirled around her slender, pale thighs, dampening her dress, now bunched around her hips.

"Set on living dangerously, are y—och, look at that! A wee seal. Or is it a selkie?" Cameron said.

Distracted she turned to look, and Cameron pounced, scooping her into his arms.

"You cheated!" But she made no move to escape him. For a long moment they simply stared into each others' eyes.

His boots were ruined, his trews soaked to the waist, but the chill of the cold seawater did nothing to quench his arousal. "I ought to drop you right in it." He made a feint, as if to drop her in the sea.

She squeaked and clung to him, laughing. "No don't, Cameron. Please."

"I thought you loved the sea."

She clung harder. "I do, but this is my only dress!"

He paused, as if making up his mind. "A forfeit then."

She narrowed her eyes. "What kind of forfeit?"

"A kiss."

"Och, well, I suppose, if I must." She gave a sigh of resignation, but her eyes were dancing and she lifted her mouth to his with a sweetness that fair pierced his soul. Her lips were cold, tangy with sea-salt but her kiss was all heat and sweet, dark-honey woman.

It was a feast of a kiss, luscious and intoxicating. He almost dropped her in the sea, forgetting himself, lost in the taste and feel of her. The little jerk as she grabbed him to save herself from falling pulled him back to awareness.

He waded out of the sea and deposited her on the sand.

They glanced at each other, then looked away, unsure of what to say—at least Cameron wasn't. The spilling over of lighthearted fun, into . . . Passion was the only word for it. It had shocked him.

He stared down at her, this slender sprite of a girl he'd married. He hardly knew her, and yet . . .

Her eyes were luminous, so blue against the shifting grays of the sea and the sky. A curlew wheeled overhead.

The silence stretched, broken only by the curlew's mournful cry and the sound of the wind and the waves. She brushed down her skirt, shaking out the wrinkles and the sand.

Still reeling from the unexpected surge of . . . feeling, Cameron took refuge in banality. He glanced at the banking clouds. "It'll probably rain later this evening."

"I'll fetch my things." She hurried up the beach, shook out the blue shawl and wrapped it around her. She picked up her shoes, hesitated and glanced at the clouds. "Must we return immediately?"

He shook his head. "There's still time for a walk if you want."

"Good." She slipped her arm through his and they started walking along the beach, Cameron squelching along in his sodden boots, Jeannie walking lightly across the sand, skipping every now and then to keep up with him, her shoes dangling from one hand.

The laird's bride, barefoot on the beach like any village urchin. It wasn't at all proper. But it felt so right.

Every now and then she stopped to pick something up, a shell, or a smooth stone, or a softly glowing piece of sea glass. She slipped them into her pocket.

"What do you want them for?" he asked, intrigued.

She shrugged. "I don't know, nothing really. They're pretty. I can't help it. I always collect things from the beach. Papa used to say I was half selkie."

"Not with those eyes, you're not."

"What's wrong with my eyes?"

"Nothing, they're perfect."

"But you said—"

"A selkie's eyes are brown, like a seal's. Your eyes are the color of the summer sky just after sunset, the brilliance of the day deepened by the coming of night." He swallowed, feeling suddenly embarrassed, and glanced at her, wondering whether she would laugh at his clumsy attempt at courting. The irony was he meant every word of it.

But she wasn't laughing. "That's beautiful, Cameron. Thank you." She hugged their linked arms closer. He could feel the slight swell of her breast pressing against him. They walked on.

"So what did you do today," she asked after a few minutes.

He told her all about the roofs they were fixing, and the new bridge he planned to build. She listened intently, and asked questions that drew him on to explain his plans for the future of the estate.

He hadn't really talked to anyone about those plans, not in detail. Uncle Charles had no interest in the welfare of those he called peasants, and as for his cousins, well, Donald might be interested, but his brother Jimmy was hopeless and would be bored by any serious talk.

It was a pleasure to test out his thoughts on someone who was interested and who asked intelligent questions. She really listened.

He suddenly remembered what Bridget had said, about courting and the importance of talking and listening. They'd almost reached the far end of the beach, and so far he'd done all the talking.

He turned for the walk back. "And how was your

day? I'm sorry I left you to manage on your own—there's no telling how long we have before the winter weather sets in. This work is urgent."

"I know, and I was fine on my own. Not that I was on my own for much of the day. In the morning, Mrs. Findlay showed me all over the castle. And then, if you recall, I had tea with your uncle."

"Aye, I'm so sorry—I meant to be with you for that. I hope it wasna too unpleasant." Uncle Charles could be quite scathing and dismissive towards those he considered his social inferiors.

She gave him a surprised look. "But it was no' unpleasant at all. He was charming and hospitable."

"Charming? And hospitable? To you?"

She laughed at his expression. "Yes, to me. I admit, I'd expected him to be hostile, but he wasn't, not a bit. In fact, he was quite sweet."

"*Sweet?*" He stared at her in disbelief. "Are we talking about the same man? Uncle Charles Sinclair, all airs and graces, direct from old Versailles, satin breeks, white powdered wig and all?"

"I admit he was a bit stiff and prickly at first, but when he found out who my father was—"

Cameron blinked. "Who your father was? Who *was* your father?"

"I told you, he was a poet. One your uncle admired." He must have looked as blank as he felt, for she added, "Remember the book of Papa's poetry? The bride gift your uncle gave me? With the blue cover?"

"Ah. Yes, yes. Of course." He hadn't really taken in the details.

"I was so touched. I didn't have a copy of my own, you see. It was a very limited printing."

"He wasn't being cutting or superior?"

"No, we had a delightful chat. He's going to paint my portrait."

Cameron shook his head in wonder. "Are you some kind of witch? An uncle-taming witch?"

She laughed. "He's really a sweet, lonely old man."

Cameron rolled his eyes. "That sweet, lonely old man nearly brought this estate to ruination with his impractical spendthrift ways." And drove him to make a hasty marriage with a woman he didn't know.

"Yes, he told me about the silk panels. But I have an idea about them that might help smooth the waters."

"We're not getting ridiculously expensive silk panels from—"

"The woman who made my beautiful shawl, I wondered if she and some of the other village women could weave and embroider some hangings to your uncle's designs."

He frowned, considering it. "It might be possible," he conceded. The more he thought about it, the more he realized what a good idea it was. Work for the village women, and a face-saving project for Uncle Charles. And affordable.

"You *are* a witch," he told Jeannie. "I've been at daggers drawn with Uncle Charles for weeks, and you arrive and within a day—a day!—you've come up with a way to soothe his ruffled feathers, *and* help some of the village women to earn some income. Winter is the perfect time for a project of this sort."

She gave a happy little skip beside him. They walked in silence for a while, then she said, "There's something else I think you should know." She told him about his housekeeper's fading sight. "Mrs. Findlay was worried you'd want to dismiss her but I promised her she could stay on."

"Oh you did, did you?"

"Aye, I did." She faced him with a martial glint in her eyes. "You told me I was to be the woman of the house, and that means I make the decisions about who works inside the house. I warn you, Cameron—"

He snorted. "Settle down, firebrand. I said it and I meant it. Run the house however you like." He took her arm and walked on, sobered by the realization that within a day his bride had found out more about his uncle and now his housekeeper than Cameron had in a six-month. It was a galling thought.

"As if I'd dismiss old Finney. The woman practically raised me. Dismiss her indeed! Why the devil didn't she tell me she was having problems seeing?"

"It must be very frightening, to be old and alone, and going blind," Jeannie said softly. "She has her pride, you know."

Cameron grunted, his own pride slightly dented. It was up to him to care for his people. "You say Finney hadn't even seen a doctor? I'll send her to Edinburgh, get her eyes checked by a specialist."

"Oh, that's a wonderful idea." Jeannie hugged his arm. "You're a fine laird, Cameron Fraser, and I'm very proud to be your wife."

"You're no' so bad yourself, Jeannie McLeay Fraser." His eyes dropped to her mouth. "But at the present moment, you're my bride, no' my wife." It was a delicate distinction. But one very much on his mind.

She swallowed. Her gaze dropped. Overhead the lone bird circled, its plaintive call echoing in the dusk.

She bent to put on her shoes, and when she straightened, he proffered his arm. She hesitated

before taking it and when she did it was a light, dec-
orous touch, not the warm hugging hold it had been
earlier.

They walked back along the beach in silence.
Cameron mentally cursed his thoughtless comment.
She was miffed with him now for pointing out the
truth.

How much longer was this blasted courtship going
to take?

Chapter Fourteen

SHE WOULD NOT feel guilty, she would not. *My bride, no' my wife.* The words had stung.

But married or not, she had a *right* to a courtship. Their marriage had given Cameron what he wanted. His inheritance had been the sole reason for his marrying, and he had full control of it now.

The very first thing he'd done, the very evening of the wedding, was to send off a flurry of orders to Inverness and more to Edinburgh, via the ship leaving at dawn the next morning. She'd overheard a couple of the servants talking about it later. Building supplies, she gathered. For rebuilding houses and the ruined bridge.

There had been no place in his plans for her, not for Jeannie McLeay with all her hopes and dreams and worries. Just for 'a wife.'

She didn't blame him for it, but she had to make space in this marriage for *her*, had to make him notice her, as she was noticing everything about him.

She admired him, she truly did, for caring for his people, for working so hard to ensure they were warm and safe from the elements over winter. He'd sacrificed himself, his own wants and possible choices, by marrying the first eligible woman he'd met.

She might have begun as an 'eligible woman', but she was determined that wasn't all she'd be.

He'd treated her with kindness and respect, but as far as she could see, he treated everyone that way. Look at how he'd reacted to the news that his housekeeper wasn't able to do her job properly.

Kindness and respect were important—Jeannie had to admit she'd had neither in the last six years with Grandad. She ought to be grateful—and she was. But kindness and respect were not enough. Jeannie wanted more.

The sea breeze picked up, sharp with the promise of winter, and Jeannie hugged her shawl around her. It was a beautiful gift—and chosen to match her eyes. She would treasure it the rest of her life.

She'd asked to be courted, and he was trying, she could see he was, with this walk, and the shawl.

What was the matter with her that she couldna' be satisfied with that?

The trouble was, when she'd stood before the minister in her borrowed dress and too-big shoes, she'd given more than her hand to Cameron Fraser. She'd tumbled head over heels for him as he stood tall and strong, so beautiful in his kilt, making sacred vows to her in a firm, deep voice.

She wanted, oh but she desperately wanted him to . . . to fall for her, too.

And not simply because he wanted to bed her.

They reached the narrow, twisty path that led up from the beach to the castle. He let her hand slip off his arm and turned to face her. "What I said before, I didna' mean it—at least I did, but it came out . . . wrong."

His eyes were steady and sincere. Drat the man, it was impossible to stay cross with him.

"The trouble is, I want you something fierce, Jeannie." He waited a moment, then added, "And I think you want me too."

Jeannie swallowed. She had nothing to say to that. Aye, she wanted him, what woman would not? But she was gambling with her future happiness here. She wanted him to know her, to feel something for her before they lay down in a bed together.

If she admitted now that she wanted him, she knew what would happen: he'd sweep away all her hesitations, and take her to bed. And then . . .

Aye, what then? She knew little about what passed between men and women, between husband and wife. But she'd heard women talking about how men, once they'd got what they wanted, lost interest.

She'd asked for a fortnight's grace, a short courtship. It wasn't much to ask. Two weeks to try to make him fall in love with her. Asking for the impossible.

He cupped her chin in his hand and tilted it until she met his gaze. "I didn'a mean to hurt your feelings," he said softly. "I'm just . . . impatient." He bent and his mouth brushed hers, a short, sweet kiss, rueful and tender. "Now, let's awa' up this path. Dinner awaits."

He took her hand in his and slid his other hand around to the small of her back. Supportive. Protective.

They climbed the path to the castle. His palm was warm against the hollow of her back. Awareness hummed between them.

After dinner he invited her to play chess. Jeannie was good at chess. She accepted with alacrity.

She lost the game, utterly unable to concentrate during those long silences during which he contemplated the chess board and she contemplated him. An unfair advantage, him being so handsome.

Thoroughly trounced and not a little embarrassed, she challenged him to a card game, which was quick and left little space for . . . gazing. They came out even.

Then it was time for bed. Jeannie went upstairs first. She washed, pulled on her nightgown, then blew out the candles, slipped between the cool sheets, and waited.

Shadows from the fire danced on the walls. Was she doing the right thing in denying him his marital rights? What if instead of getting closer, he was getting frustrated? Was she driving him to seek the company of other women? This widow, Bridget, who made beautiful shawls, perhaps.

She turned over in the bed, trying to shut off the questions in disgust. When had she become such a ditherer? It had taken her a bare few minutes to agree to marry him.

But back then her choice had been easy; she had nothing to lose. Now . . .

Och! She turned over again. It was impossible, her body at war with her brain. And where was her heart in all this? Aching and uncertain, that's where.

The door opened and Cameron entered. Jeannie lay there, feigning sleep, trying to decide what to do, as she listened to the sounds of him undressing. She felt the mattress dip as he slid into the bed behind her.

Gently he pulled her closer and tucked her against him, his arm around her waist. Her back rested against his chest, her bottom was snuggled tight into the angle of his body. His warmth soaked into her. His arousal pressed against her. Silently insistent.

The clean, masculine smell of him surrounded her. She breathed it in deeply. It was addictive. He was addictive. Her body softened against him, pliant, unable to resist.

Should she turn over and tell him yes? Get it over with and stop this dreadful uncertainty? Did she really need a courtship?

She opened her mouth to tell him yes, when out of the darkness he murmured, "Relax, hen, I canna help the way my body reacts to you. Just ignore it and go to sleep. I'll no' bother you."

The following morning Jeannie woke alone in the big bed. She supposed it was something she'd have to get used to.

She told herself he was to be admired, getting up at dawn—before dawn, for all she knew—in order to repair other people's roofs. A man who worked so hard to ensure the welfare of his people would be a good husband as well as a good laird.

Still, it would have been nice sometimes, to wake together, to lie side by side in that big warm bed and plan the day together. And maybe a good-morning kiss.

And whose fault was it that the man had no inclination to linger in bed?

My bride, not my wife.

Over the next few days a routine developed. Jeannie spent the mornings supervising the household, learning Mrs. Findlay's system, making decisions with Cook, and getting to know the various members of the household. And giving the castle a good spring clean. She was determined to get the castle spotless.

Mrs. Findlay, her pride stung by the inadvertent neglect caused by her approaching blindness, was in an equally militant frame of mind and she ruthlessly harried the maids and menservants, keeping them sweeping and scrubbing, dusting and polishing all day. Jeannie, too was everywhere, supervising, advising and even joining in the housework from time to time, wrapped in a large white apron that she'd borrowed, much to Mrs. Findlay's disapproval.

"You're the laird's wife, no' a maidservant!" she'd told Jeannie when she caught her helping one of the maids take down some dusty curtains for washing. "An apron is for a servant to wear!"

But Jeannie didn't see the point in standing around waiting for another pair of hands to arrive when her own were perfectly capable. And she wasn't going to risk dirtying her only dress. There was still no sign of any village seamstress. Never mind an apron, at this rate she'd end up borrowing a dress from her maid.

In the afternoons she would remove the apron, tidy herself and take tea with Uncle Charles. He wasn't the enemy she'd imagined when Cameron first told of his reasons for their hurried marriage. The man was lonely, she realized. And to fill his empty days he'd dreamed of making this castle more like Versailles, as he had done to his own rooms. He was a dreamer, like her father, totally impractical, but no real threat to Cameron or herself.

They would talk about art and poetry, and he'd tell her tales of his youth in Paris, rose-tinted memories, for the most part, she was sure. Several times she slipped in a suggestion about hangings for the hall, but though he nodded politely enough, he would always change the subject, and talk instead of his plans to paint her portrait.

But the highlight of Jeannie's day always came when Cameron arrived home. He'd wash away the dust of the day and come to her, his hair still damp and clinging to his forehead in clumps. A man to take her breath away.

"A walk, my lady?" He'd present his arm, and she'd take it eagerly, and off they'd go on a long walk, a different path every time.

The day after their beach walk, he took her to a different part of the coast, a rocky outcrop, with deep rock pools. She slipped on a piece of seaweed and nearly fell in, but he grabbed her and pulled her hard against him.

They stood for a long moment, breast to chest, gazing into each other's eyes. Jeannie breathed in the scent of him, reveling in the warmth and strength of his big hard body, the feel of his arms wrapped around her.

"That was close," he said eventually. He stepped back, releasing her, and the cold breeze off the sharp, briny sea was like a slap against her skin. "You might have been washed away. The tides are strong here."

"I can swim." The heat in his eyes flustered her, but he simply took her hand as if nothing had happened, and they walked on.

Jeannie then told him about growing up on the isle of Lewis, of the brilliant turquoise of the water in summer, and the way the autumn mists could creep in, soft and uncanny, and how in winter the island could be lashed by wild storms. And how after the storm had passed, the birds would return, and only then would you realize they'd gone silent, and you'd wonder where they'd been.

Babbling, she was, because all she really wanted to talk about was the meaning of that silent, burning look he'd given her.

But it was clear he didn't want to talk about it, so instead she talked of beaches and rock pools, and the sea-treasures she'd collected over the years; the shells and glass and pieces of beautifully twisted and sanded driftwood.

He laughed. "By the time we're old, the castle will be half buried in pretty shells and sea glass."

By the time we're old. It warmed her to think of that, a home with Cameron. And maybe children. A family to love and belong to again.

She told him about her father's passion for poetry. "He was a dreamer, Da, and we lived from hand to mouth—he was always looking for a patron, and could never keep a job for long. But he was the sweetest, kindest man, and Mam and I loved him dearly." Jeannie 's voice broke then, and Cameron squeezed her hand and they walked on.

"Mam was the practical one. In the end she went out and got herself a position in a great house. And oh, the quarrel over that! Da was all, 'My wife doesna work!' He was brought up soft, you see—a gentleman—but Mam, she'd grown up with Grandad. Hard work didn't frighten her."

"Or you," Cameron observed quietly. "So what did your mother say to that?"

She laughed. "That we either starved genteelly or she could get a job! And that was the end of that! They took her on as a housemaid but after a few years she rose to being the housekeeper. Decisive, well-organized and a wee bit bossy, that was Mam."

She stooped to pick a handful of long-stalked feathery grass. She liked picking wild sprigs of green and pretty grasses for the castle. Greenery softened the stone.

"I learned a lot from her about running a great house," Jeannie reflected, "but if I'd known I'd one day be the wife of a laird, I'd've paid a lot more attention."

"You're doing fine, lass. The house is looking grand and half the staff is wrapped around your little finger."

"Only half?" she joked, and he chuckled.

His appreciation pleased her, but she wanted more than appreciation from him. But it was early days yet, and he was honoring his promise and giving her what she'd asked for—a courtship. And oh, it was grand getting to know him, and he her.

He showed her a pretty glen with lacy, bare-branched trees and arching ferns and a narrow burn running down the middle. The water burbled noisily over the rocks and he took her hand in his, and helped her carefully across.

Jeannie loved the feel of his hands, big and strong and slightly calloused from the work he was doing. No soft-skinned gentleman he.

"We built a dam here once, when I was a lad, my cousins and me," he told her. "It started out as a plan to trap fish, but stacking rocks is dull work, and well, boys and water." He flashed her a crooked grin, his teeth gleaming white in the soft, dim evening. "Somehow it turned into a Viking battle. We came home well after dark, drenched to the skin, and mud and bruises all over." He chuckled softly. "Did we ever get into trouble. But it was a grand battle, and well worth a whipping."

They walked on, hand in hand. Through the delicate tracery of branches, the sky turned from gold to lilac, slowly deepening to a velvety indigo. It was magic. Silent footsteps on a fragrant carpet of moss and leaf litter, quiet voices accompanied by the musical burbling of the burn.

He told her of the day his mother had died. He'd been a wee lad at the time, and his memories of her were faint. Mostly he remembered her perfume. Mrs. Findlay and Cook had brought him up, he said. And his Da.

He told her about his father, and how he'd also died, too young, when Cameron was but a stripling. And then Uncle Ian, who'd taken the place of his father.

So much death in Cameron's life. They had that in common.

They were a gift Jeannie savored, these precious times alone with her husband, just the two of them walking and talking in the quiet hush of the evening, with the sky turning gold and rose and violet overhead.

Her footsteps always slowed as they neared the castle. She never wanted their walks to end. She was coming to understand her husband more now, and she hoped he felt the same about her. But would they still do this once her courtship was over? A little over a week to go now. Such a short time.

Chapter Fifteen

THE FOLLOWING DAY, Jeannie was working with a couple of maids, cleaning out one of the upstairs chambers when she glanced out of the window and noticed something of a procession coming from the direction of the harbor. Men, and horses pulling carts, laden with lumber and boxes and mysterious bundles in various shapes and sizes.

One of the housemaids peeped over her shoulder. "Och, that'll be the boat."

"The boat?" Jeannie queried.

"Aye, bringin' all the supplies the laird sent for when he got back from—er, when he returned with you, m'lady, married. He sent off a great long order that very night." She added with satisfaction. "He'll be able to get all the repairs done now, and start on the new bridge."

"Oh, good." Building supplies. That would make him happy. Jeannie turned back to her work.

A short time later the housekeeper appeared in the doorway. There was an air of suppressed excitement about her. "Would you please step up to your bed-chamber, m'lady?"

"My bedchamber? Why? What's the problem?"

"You'll see when you get there," the housekeeper

said austerely. "Now come awa' wi' ye—and take off that apron. And there's a smut on your nose."

Mystified, Jeannie removed the apron and wiped her face, then hurried off to her bedchamber, followed by the housekeeper.

She entered the bedchamber and stopped dead. A small, dark, quietly elegant woman—a complete stranger—stood there with Mairie, her maid, and the neat, bare room Jeannie had left that morning was now a riot of color and texture.

Every available surface was draped with clothing; dresses in blues, greens, lilac, crimson, creamy yellow and more, patterned and plain, in silk, satin, linen and wool. On the bed lay mounds of what looked like underclothes; petticoats in fine lawn, bodices, camisoles—even drawers—all trimmed with lace and finer than anything Jeannie had ever worn.

"Wh—what is all this?" she stammered. And who was the strange lady who stood so quietly watching?

"It's the laird," Mairie said excitedly. "He ordered all this for you. It came in the boat with the other supplies—"

"From Madame Fouchet's, the finest dressmaker in Edinburgh," Mrs. Findlay added. She gestured to the small lady standing quietly by. "And this is one of her seamstresses, Mme—"

"Dubois," the lady said, and curtseyed. "How do you do, my lady. Madame Fouchet sent me to attend to the correct fitting of all the garments. They are not quite finished and will need some personal adjustments, *non*?"

Jeannie didn't know what to say. He'd ordered her all these beautiful dresses? Considering her needs when she'd thought he only had building supplies on his mind?

Dazed, she picked up one of the dresses at the top of the pile and held it against her. It was a simple day dress in a soft blue fabric patterned with tiny yellow flowers. A scooped neck, three quarter length sleeves and flaring out from a 'waistline' that sat high under the bosom—was this the fashion in Edinburgh, then? She gazed at her reflection in the looking glass. "It's so pretty," she breathed.

The little seamstress bustled forward. "Try it on, my lady, and we shall make the adjustments necessary. You wish to wear it at once?"

Jeannie did. For the next hour she tried on dress after dress, with Mm. Dubois tweaking and muttering in French and making notes, all with a dozen or more pins in her mouth.

The dresses fitted almost perfectly. "How did you know to get such a good fit?" she asked.

Mairie laughed. "The laird asked me to tak' the measurements of that dress you wore that first night—remember, I took it awa' for cleaning? And Mrs. Findlay and I made a list of everything we thought you might need. There's a shoemaker as well, waiting downstairs."

Jeannie was dazzled by the forethought and consideration her husband had shown, all without a word to her. And then she realized something. "So is this why the village seamstress was unable to help me out? And why there was such a shortage of ready-made homespun available? Because you knew this"—she gestured to the sumptuous pile—"would be coming in a few days."

Mairie giggled, and Mrs. Findlay nodded. "The

laird's wife doesn'a wear homespun," she said simply.

And that was that.

For the rest of the afternoon Jeannie stood, slowly circling while the lovely new dresses were tweaked and pinned and tacked. Mme. Dubois was adamant that everything must fit 'just so.'

Then while the Frenchwoman was sewing, a neat little man was shown up. He, too had some half-finished slippers ready to be fitted on her and a pair of brown half boots that, amazingly, were a perfect fit.

By the end of the day Jeannie stood in front of the looking glass, breathless. The first new dress she'd had in years, and oh, it was so soft and pretty. Mairie and Mme. Dubois had dressed her hair in a sophisticated style, and from somewhere, the Frenchwoman had produced a handful of tiny yellow silk flowers that they'd woven into her hair.

She looked like a proper lady.

She couldn't wait for Cameron to see her. "He's coming, m'lady." Mairie had been keeping watch for him. "He'll be inside in two minutes."

Jeannie hurried to the head of the stairs and waited. She felt it the moment he saw her. He stopped dead, staring up at her, and the expression in his eyes set her heart a'thumping.

She swallowed and took a deep breath. She'd planned a dignified glide down the stairs in her new shoes and her new dress, acting every inch the lady.

But she couldn't restrain herself. "Thank you, oh, thank you Cameron. I didn't think you'd realize—I never imagined you'd—but you did—and oh, have you ever seen anything so pretty—and there's more upstairs—you must have spent a fortune, and oh, you shouldn't have, but I'm so happy you did—so many beautiful dresses—and the shoes—so dainty and yet a perfect fit—how did you know?" The words tumbled out of her, and the faster she spoke, the faster she moved until by the time she reached the bottom of the steps she was running. She flew across the floor and flung herself into his open arms.

Laughing, he swung her around in a circle and when he finally stopped, he cupped her face in both hands and gave her a kiss that practically dissolved her knees.

"I'm glad you like your new clothes, wife," he said, and she blushed, realizing that half the castle had witnessed her mad rush down the stairs, babbling like a loon and hurling herself at their laird. They were all clapping and laughing.

She clung to him dizzily. So much for a dignified ladylike entrance. And as for that kiss . . . Her cheeks were on fire.

"I think we'll walk through the village tonight," he said quietly. "Show off my bonny bride in her bonny new dress. What say you? Are you ready to meet my people?"

———

It was dusk by the time they returned. Cameron, to honor the occasion—and to underline his message to his people—had changed into the kilt he'd worn at his wedding. He fancied they made a fine sight, the laird and his lady, strolling through the village.

At his side, Jeannie was very quiet. "They're all very friendly, aren't they?" she said. "So kind and welcoming."

"Of course. Why wouldn't they be?" His people's welcome of his bride was on his behalf at this stage, but once they got to know her, they'd love her, he was sure.

She grimaced. "I'll never remember all their names."

"You will, in time."

She squeezed his arm. "Thank you for waiting until I was fit to be seen."

He frowned. He wasn't ashamed of how she looked when he first brought her home—Lord, did she not know how bonny she was? "You'd be bonny wearing nothing but a wheat bag," he told her and was rewarded with a blush and a glowing look.

As they neared the castle entrance, they heard the sound of someone roaring and bellowing in the courtyard. "Oh no!" Jeannie exclaimed, and sped toward the noise, fleet as a young doe.

Cameron raced after her. What the hell was she doing, running *toward* trouble?

He entered the courtyard a few steps behind her, and saw the source of the commotion, a tall rangy man of about sixty, with wild gray hair. It was clear the man had been drinking. He was reeling and staggering and bellowing at the top of his voice, "Gi' me back ma granddaughter! Stolen awa' from me, she was! Where is she? Where's the bastard that took her?"

Folk stood in small clumps, watching warily from a distance.

Before Cameron could stop her, Jeannie marched up and confronted the man. "Hush your shouting, Grandad. I was *not* stolen! I left of my own free will, as you very well know."

He swung unsteadily around to face her and scanned her up and down, taking in her fashionable dress, the yellow flowers, her blue shawl. The look on his face darkened. "Look at you in your fancy clothes, flaunting your bosom before the world, ye shameless wee hoor! Ye're coming hame wi' me, where ye belong." He reached out to grab her but Jeannie, anticipating the move, skipped out of reach.

She glanced at Cameron, and made a gesture for him to stay back, saying in a low voice, "He's *my* grandfather. I'll handle him."

Cameron gave her a curt nod and stepped back, glowering. It went against the grain to leave this drunken bastard to her. Ewan Leith was a dour, bitter, bad-tempered man who'd taken the poorest of care of his young orphaned granddaughter—out on the hills with the sheep in all weather, clothed in rags and keeping her half starved with his miserly ways.

He itched for an excuse to give Leith the hiding he deserved. But he was an older man, and Jeannie's only living relative. If she wanted to deal with him, he would respect that. To a point.

"Calm down, Grandad, I'm perfectly well, as you can see. But I'm no' coming home wi' ye." She spoke calmly, reasonably—trying to put a good face on it for the sake of their audience, Cameron realized. Acting as though her grandfather had come out of concern for her. He doubted anyone was fooled.

The old man scowled. "Who's goin' to cook for me, then? Who'll mind the sheep?"

"You can cook for yourself. *You* can mind the sheep," she said evenly. "You did it before I came to live with you, and you can do it now."

"Ye shameless wee besom — ye *owe* it to me. You have a, a *duty* to me. I'm your *grandfather!*"

"I know. But I'm a married woman now, Grandad, and I have a duty to my husband."

Cameron watched, ready to jump in if necessary, but proud of the cool way Jeannie was handling the man, not entering into his argument, but firmly restating her position. Aye, she was going to make a grand laird's lady. He could see from the expressions on his people's faces that they thought the same.

Ewen Leith snorted. He peered past Jeannie, to where Cameron stood by, arms folded. "Ye're the one who stole her away, are ye?"

"I'm the man who *married* her. Cameron Fraser, laird of this castle."

"Ye had nae right. She's mine, my only grandchild. She belongs tae *me*!" He gestured dramatically at his chest and staggered a few steps backwards.

"Nonsense! I'm of an age to make my own decisions," Jeannie said briskly. "Now, I'm married and I'm no' going back, so stop this fuss and come along inside and have a nice cup of tea and something to eat." She went to take his arm and lead him inside, but he flung her off violently, almost knocking her to the ground.

Cameron caught her before she fell. He set her carefully aside, then turned and poked her grandfather hard in the chest. "Lay a finger on my wife again, old man, and I'll not be answerable for the consequences."

"Your *wife*," Leith sneered. "She's nothing but a hoor, you'll see. Running after any man she finds. She'll lie down with any man who asks her. I know, I've seen what she got up to in the hills when she thought I wasna watching."

Jeannie gasped with indignation. A murmur ran through the watching castle folk.

Cameron's fist flew out and hit Leith on the jaw with a crack that sent the old man staggering. "That's a filthy lie and you know it, you evil-minded old miser. My wife came to her marriage bed a virgin."

He reached out and drew Jeannie to his side in a quick one-armed hug. He glanced at the listening crowd and added, "As the sheets testified."

He let that sink in, then added, "One more word, Leith, and I'll beat you to a pulp. Grandfather or not, *no-one* disrespects my wife." He stepped back, breathing heavily.

Jeannie clutched his arm. Cameron glanced down at her worried face and leashed his anger. The man might be a miserable cur, but he was her only living relative. "If you care to return in a more respectful frame of mind, Leith—and when you're no' the worse for drink—you'll be welcome to visit. But for now, you're no' welcome in my—in *our* home."

Leith made a rude sound "You couldna pay me to come here again." He turned and marched unsteadily away.

"Grandad," Jeannie called.

He hesitated, then stopped and looked back.

"If you're ever in need, you will always have a place here," she told him. "Family is family."

His face twisted in scorn. "Family? Ye're no part of me! Ye're as useless and lazy and wicked as your mother was!" He stumped away.

Jeannie said softly, "Everybody loved Mam. But who loves you, Grandad?"

Chapter Sixteen

THE OLD MAN staggered off out of view and, the show over, the watching crowd dispersed. Cameron wrapped an arm around his wife's slender waist and squeezed. "You handled him very well."

She was shaking. "I don't know about that—he's always been bitter and morose and impossible to please—but thank you for letting me try."

He pulled her closer. "Forget the cup of tea, how about a wee dram before dinner? Settle your nerves."

She nodded and they entered the castle together, his arm wrapped firmly around her waist.

Having met her grandfather, Cameron now had a clearer understanding of why, that day on the causeway, in the mud and the bleak surrounds, a young girl would accept a marriage proposal from a man she didn't know.

She'd had nothing to lose.

It wasn't exactly flattering.

Jeannie had disrobed and washed, and was waiting in her nightgown by the fire, snuggled in her favorite blue shawl when Cameron came up to bed.

"Something wrong?" he asked.

"No, I just wanted to thank you."

"For what?"

"For letting me handle Grandad."

In the middle of pulling off his coat, he turned and quirked a brow at her. "Did you no' notice that rather fine punch I landed on the man?"

She rose from her chair, and stood before him, clutching the shawl tightly around her. "Aye, but you let me try first." He hadn't pushed her aside as if it were men's business, hadn't made her look weak in front of all those watching people.

She swallowed. "And I want to thank you for, for what you said. About . . . " She felt her cheeks heating, and swallowed. "For defending my virtue the way you did." So firmly and publicly.

He shrugged as if it were of little account. "You're my wife."

"But I'm no', am I? Not yet. And yet you declared in front of my grandfather and half the village that I came to my marriage bed a virgin."

He said nothing, just pulled his shirt off over his head and tossed it on a chair, then sat down on it to pull off his boots.

"You had no way of knowing it was true."

He snorted. "Aye, I did."

She frowned, puzzled. "How could you know? We haven't . . . " She glanced at the bed.

He stood to undo his breeches, dropped them and came to her in nothing but his drawers. He looked down at her, cupped her chin in his big warm hand and said gruffly, "Och, lass, the innocence of you shines from those bonny blue eyes. And in this . . . " He bent and kissed her, his mouth firm, warm. Possessive.

The taste of him, hot, spicy, masculine, was like a spark to dry tinder. She leaned into him, wanting more, and twined her arms around his neck as he teased her lips apart and took possession of her mouth. He gathered her hard against him, deepening the kiss. Heat rose from his body. Heat and a clean, masculine scent that she inhaled hungrily.

She heard a little humming noise, and realized it was coming from her, and then she forgot everything, except the taste and feel and scent of him.

She stroked her palms blindly over his skin, over his chest, and his arms, enthralled by the feel of his firm, masculine flesh. Ripples of sensation poured through her, her knees weakened and she clung to him.

And then, abruptly he released her—put her away from him and stepped back, breathing heavily. She reached for the bed post and held onto it; her legs were all jelly. She, too was panting. "Wh-what's wrong?"

He gave a raspy laugh. "Nothing's wrong, It's just . . . I gave you my word."

She blinked stupidly at him, her senses still in turmoil.

"You asked for two weeks' grace, remember? For courtship."

"Oh." Her gaze dropped to the front of his drawers, where some interesting action seemed to be happening.

"Yes, 'oh'." He turned away from her and stared out of the window. "So hop into bed now, and go to sleep. I'll join you in a wee while."

"But—"

"I shouldna have started something I canna finish." She hesitated, and he added in a hard voice, "Bed, Jeannie. I'll no' ask you again."

She bit her lip, and climbed into the bed. If

he'd asked her a moment ago, while she was blissful in his arms, she would have said yes to him,
wouldn't have thought twice about it. But he'd given
his word, and he was a man who prided himself on
never breaking it.

She was hot and rumpled and her body was sticky,
and humming with a deep restless hunger. She
wanted him something fierce, but she climbed into
bed without a word and lay there, feigning sleep.

A good while later she felt him climb in beside her,
but he didn't touch her, not this time. There would
be no big warm body curled around her tonight.

What madness had caused her to ask for a fortnight? Her body ached for him now.

<hr />

The next morning, alone again in the big bed,
Jeannie lay thinking about decorative hangings for
the hall, and the village women she'd now met, particularly Bridget, who'd made Jeannie's beautiful
shawl. Recently widowed and with a brood of bairns
to feed, Bridget wasn't the only widow with bairns.
They needed to earn money.

But Uncle Charles was dragging his feet. He was
simply indulging her, she decided. He had no faith in
the ability of the local women to achieve his vision
or meet his superior standards.

Time to bite the bullet. After breakfast she sent
Mairie out with a message to invite the best weavers
in the village to take tea with herself and the old
gentleman that very afternoon, and to bring their
finest weavings with them. They came, but instead
of the enthusiasm Jeannie expected, she found herself facing quiet resistance.

The women, dressed in their Sunday best, were
polite but reserved, speaking only when spoken to,

barely nibbling on the biscuits and cakes Cook had prepared. None of them made a move to bring out their weavings, even when she invited them to lay them out on the side-table.

The old gentleman didn't make it any easier for her either, acting very much The Nobleman deigning to meet with Peasants, an attitude Jeannie hoped the women would forgive. Or at least overlook.

But it was hard going.

After the tea had been served, and laborious conversation made, Jeannie marshaled her courage and addressed them all. "Thank you for coming. As some of you have seen, I'm doing what I suppose most new brides do, making over my husband's home." A few women nodded, grateful for the extra work her activities had provided.

She continued, "But stone walls make for a cold home, and I'd like to remedy that. This beautiful shawl that Mrs. Fraser made is so lovely." She smoothed the blue shawl around her shoulders. "I understand you are all excellent weavers, and I'm sure you've all heard of what a fine artist the laird's uncle, Mr. Sinclair, is. So I thought, if we put the two together . . ." She explained her vision of the project, a series of wall hangings designed by Uncle Charles and woven by the women.

While she spoke, Uncle Charles sat back, buffing his nails in a bored manner and sighing from time to time in a world-weary manner, making it clear that this project was not his idea. And that she was casting pearls before swine.

Jeannie felt like strangling him, but forced herself to continue brightly on. When she'd finished, there was a long silence.

Finally one of the women cleared her throat. "'Tis

a grand idea, my lady, but the thing is, most of us already sell our weavings in Edinburgh. And all *our own* designs." From the way she was pointedly not looking at Uncle Charles, it was clear she was less than impressed with his airs and graces.

Uncle Charles sat up. "In *Edinburgh?*"

"Aye," Bridget Fraser joined in. "To a fine, exclusive shop down there. *And* they pay us in cash." She glanced at Uncle Charles.

Jeannie said quickly, "Och, did I not mention that we'll be paying in cash, too—and at a better rate than the man in Edinburgh." Cameron had told her about that, and mentioned he planned to see if he could improve the women's terms of trade.

"*What* shop in Edinburgh?" Uncle Charles demanded.

When Bridget told him his frown deepened. "I don't believe it." He turned to Jeannie and added in a voice quite audible to the women, "I know that establishment. It's elegant and exclusive and would *never* stock village crafts."

His comment caused a ripple of muttering among the women.

"Perhaps you're a little out of touch, Uncle Charles," Jeannie said diplomatically. "Fashions change, as you know"—she avoided glancing at his attire, which had been fashionable last century—"and Cameron told me these ladies are among the finest weavers in Scotland."

She turned to the women with a smile. "Why not show Mr. Sinclair and me some of the beautiful pieces that Edinburgh ladies flock to buy?"

Suddenly the women were eager to show off their wares. All in a spirit of defiance. Uncle Charles's skepticism and snobbery had fired them up.

Out they tumbled from baskets and bags; shawls, scarves, blankets, cushions, hangings, all in gorgeous jewel colors, some with simple, elegant designs, some a bold riot of intricate patterns. They took Jeannie's breath away.

Uncle Charles stiffened, then, unable to help himself he came forward and examined some of the pieces, fingering the fine weave, turning them over to examine the back, draping the fabric this way and that. His interest visibly grew; he couldn't hide it.

He separated out half a dozen weavings. "These might be acceptable for the hall," he told Jeannie.

"*Acceptable?* I'll have you know—"one of the women began.

"I think these are destined for Edinburgh, Uncle Charles," Jeannie interjected hastily. "We'll discuss the hangings later, if any of these ladies are interested."

The women folded up their pieces, packed them back into baskets and bundles, and returned to their seats. Jeannie served a fresh round of tea. When they'd finished, she said, "So, would any of you be willing to work with Mr. Sinclair and me to bring some warmth and color to these cold stone walls. At a price to be agreed, of course."

The women exchanged glances. There was a long silence.

Uncle Charles was the sticking point, Jeannie knew, but she was determined to give him a project to work on, and to coax him out of his isolation. And to give the village women a chance to earn money. And to make her home a warmer, more welcoming place.

She waited.

Finally Bridget spoke. "With his own hands the

laird worked to give me back my home again. I'll not deny his bride her wish. I'll make two hangings for you, my lady—one to whatever pattern Mr. Sinclair there comes up with. The second will be a piece to my own design. I will accept payment for the first, but the second will be my gift to the laird's bride."

A lump rose in Jeannie's throat. "Thank you, Mrs. Fraser," she managed. "I am most grateful for your generosity."

Bridget Fraser smiled back at her. "I remember what it was like to be a new bride, wanting to make a house into a home," she said softly. The sentiment, coming from a black clad, still-grieving widow, seemed to prompt the others.

Another woman spoke up gruffly. "Aye, I'll do the same — one of my ain pieces as a gift, and another to Mr. Sinclair's design. For cash."

One by one each of the others joined in, offering one weaving, unique and personal, for a bride gift, and a second to be made in conjunction with Uncle Charles, for cash.

By the end, Jeannie's eyes were blurry with tears. The castle was going to be drowning in woven hangings, and it would be all the warmer and more beautiful for it.

For Jeannie, it was already a warmer and more beautiful place. After so many lonely years with only Grandad, Rab the dog, and the sheep to talk to, these women had just offered her acceptance. And the beginning of friendship.

Chapter Seventeen

THE SKY WAS leaden, and bruised-looking clouds were building as Cameron arrived home. It would rain soon. So much for his planned evening walk with his bride.

The expectant looks of his servants when he stepped inside each day had prompted Cameron to notice the changes in his home, the rearranged furniture, the well beaten rugs. And if he didn't notice, someone always managed to tell him, discreetly, so he could comment. He appreciated it. His wife had been working hard, he knew.

But though the place seemed fresher and brighter, that wasn't what drew him. Knowing Jeannie was here, waiting for him at the end of each day, it gave him a feeling in his heart, made him feel more welcome, somehow, as if the castle was more of a home, even though he'd lived here all his life.

"My wife?" he asked a servant as he handed over his coat.

"Up away yonder." The man indicated the direction with his chin.

Cameron took the stairs two at a time. He was glad now he'd stopped to gather a bunch of heather. He'd felt a bit silly riding home with the flowers clutched in his hand. His cousins Jimmy and Donald had split their sides laughing when they'd seen him.

They'd learn. A man changed when he took a wife.

He opened the door to their bedchamber quietly, hoping to surprise her, but it was Cameron who got the surprise.

In front of the fire sat Jeannie in the enamel bath-tub, humming softly as she soaped herself. His mouth dried. Her hair was pinned up, exposing the lovely line of her neck and spine. Damp curls clustered around her ears and caressed her nape. Flames from the fire danced, gilding her skin.

He must have made some sort of noise, for she turned suddenly.

Slender body, all ribs, topped with lush little breasts.

"Cameron!" She snatched up the washcloth and made an attempt to cover herself. It didn't cover nearly as much as she'd hoped.

He didn't move. She was his wife.

"Cameron!" she said again, blushing furiously. "A little privacy if you please."

He shut the door, doing his best to hide a grin. Lord, but she looked good enough to eat, all pink and cream and slick and soft. "There now, we're alone." Her blush went all the way down, he was interested to see.

"Go *away*!" She was half flustered, half cross. Her nipples, beneath the inadequate washcloth were hard and pointed. Aye, she was as aroused as he was. But not wanting to admit it.

He put the flowers down, leaned against the door jamb, and waited. That water was going to get cold, eventually. She was his wife of more than a week and he hadn't yet seen her fully naked.

She glared at him. "Cameron Fraser, you're *no'* going to stand there watching me in my bath!"

He didn't move. His smile grew.

"It's . . . it's indecent."

He shrugged. "We're married."

She made a small annoyed sound, and turned her back on him in a watery flounce. Water sloshed onto the floor.

"Och, you want me to wash your back, do ye? Why didn't ye say so?"

"No, I don't—don't come any—" she began, but it was too late.

In two strides he crossed the room and squatted down behind her. She smelled delicious, like roses and vanilla. He held out his hand. "Going to pass me the soap and washcloth, or am I going to have to fish around for them?"

She turned her head to stare at him. "You wouldn't."

He grinned and rolled up his sleeves.

"Here then." She tossed the wet wash cloth at his face.

He caught it with a laugh. "Soap?"

She squirmed around, trying to find the soap with one hand while at the same time keeping her breasts covered. An altogether impossible task, Cameron was pleased to note. Lord, but she was pretty.

He soaped up the wash cloth—it smelled of roses—and began to rub her back, firm, long strokes that reached from her nape to her small soft bottom. For the first few minute she sat stiffly, hunched over, embarrassed and resistant, but he kept up the steady soothing strokes and slowly he felt her begin to unwind under his touch.

After a few minutes he unobtrusively dropped the washcloth, soaped up his hands and smoothed them over her silky skin, kneading and caressing.

He was going to have to feed her up; she was so thin he could feel every bone. That wretched grandfather of hers . . . He should have been looking after her, not sending her out on the hills to work like a man, and keeping her half-starved.

He massaged her neck and shoulders and before long she was arching against his hands, letting out small sighs and moans of pleasure, like a little cat purring. He swallowed a groan.

It was all he could do not to snatch her out of the water, toss her on the bed and have his way with her.

"Ohh, that's lovely. We worked hard today," she murmured. "I decided to clean out the cellars this afternoon. I'm a little stiff."

Cameron blinked. He was a lot stiff. But her words jerked him back to reality. He'd promised her two weeks. Dammit. His fingers moved automatically, kneading, stroking, unknotting her muscles.

He wished she would unknot his.

But he'd given his word. Like a fool. And now. . . What the hell was he going to do when she finally stood up, naked and sweet, her skin all pink and gold and gleaming wet in the firelight? Testing his control to the limit.

He should have shut himself on the outside of the door when she'd asked.

He could only think of one possible ending to this scene: in bed. And not sleeping.

"The water's getting cold," she said quietly. "I'm getting out now."

Cameron swallowed. He straightened, wiped his hands on his breeks, and only then noticed a towel draped over the chair. He handed it to her.

She didn't move. "Cameron, please."

Aye, he was embarrassing her. He strode to the window and gazed out, giving her space to stand and dry herself and hide all those sweet curves from him. His innocent, flustered little bride.

He stared out into the darkening sky, seeing nothing, imagining a slender creamy nymph rising naked from her bath.

"No weather for walking in tonight." He jumped as she spoke, almost in his ear.

She was dressed in her nightgown, with a robe wrapped around her, covered from top to small bare toes, except for a small vee of creamy skin at the neck. All he could think of was how he wanted to peel that clothing off her and take her to bed.

He swallowed hard, battling with his insistent desire. She was looking past him out of the window, and he belatedly noticed the rain pelting against the window. "No."

She rose on tiptoe and kissed his cheek. "Thank you for respecting me, Cameron."

He blinked and mumbled something.

She smiled. "And for the massage." She rose on her toes again and this time kissed him on the mouth. Warm. Lush. Open-mouthed and welcoming. Twining her arms around his neck.

He pulled her against him, hard, and sank into the kiss, deepening it, tasting her, claiming her, relishing the sweet, heady intoxication of her, his blood roaring.

She pulled away. "Cameron," she whispered, smiling and flustered. "The door."

"Eh?"

She slipped from his embrace. "There's someone at the door. To take away the bath and bathwater." He blinked, and she added, "I rang for them when I got out of the bath. I didn't know we'd . . ." She gestured with vague and endearing self-consciousness. "You know."

He knew all right. He strode to the door, and jerked it open. Two menservants and his wife's maid, Mairie entered. He waited as they carried the bath—still full—carefully away. Mairie fluttered around tidying things until he said, "That's enough. Tell Cook we'll tak' our supper up here this evening."

Mairie's eyes widened. She glanced at her mistress and blushed. "Oh, aye, Laird. " She backed out of the room, hiding a smile.

"Eat it here? But what about the others?" Jeannie said when the maid had gone. "Your cousins and your uncle, for instance?"

He shrugged. He fancied a little private conversation with his bride, and could do without the distraction of his relatives. "They can eat wherever they like."

She gave him a doubtful glance, then her gaze fell on the flowers. "Oh, are they for me?" She hurried over and picked them up. "You brought me heather. I didn't think there'd be any still in flower. Thank you, Cameron." Quite as if it was some grand expensive gift he'd brought her, and not some common flower off the hillside.

She inhaled the perfume with a blissful expression. "Such a beautiful, delicate fragrance. Smell it." She held it out to him, as if he'd never in his life smelled the flowers that bloomed in the hills all around his home. He sniffed dutifully. It smelled the same as always.

"And oh, look! There's a wee sprig of white heather." She showed it to him, her eyes shining.

"Aye, well, it's said to be good luck for a bride," he muttered, a little embarrassed by her open delight. It had been spotting the white heather that had inspired him to gather the rest.

She found a glass to hold the flowers and arranged them to her satisfaction, then took the little sprig of white heather and tucked it into her hair. Against her shining chestnut locks it looked prettier than any hair ornament.

"I used to wear a sprig of dried white heather when I was a lad," he began, then broke off, hearing a knock at the door.

A couple of servants brought supper in on a large tray, along with a bottle of wine and two glasses. They placed them on a side table, then, at a jerk of the head from Cameron, left quickly, closing the door behind them.

Chapter Eighteen

"WE'LL EAT IN front of the fire, the way I sometimes did as a wee boy."

Jeannie arranged dishes on a cloth in front of the hearth. Chicken and mushroom pie, the crust golden and flaky, cabbage and greens stewed with bacon pieces, and mashed neeps, steaming and fragrant. And for after, tucked under a cloth was a steamed rhubarb and apple pudding and a pot of thick clotted cream to top it off.

She sat back and surveyed the feast. "We'll never get through all this."

"Don't you bet on it." Cameron poured the wine. "I'm hungry enough to eat a horse."

They ate then, in silence, the only sound the clink of cutlery against crockery, the crackling of the fire and the rain drumming against the window panes. But it was a comfortable silence, Jeannie reflected as she ate the delicious supper.

Cameron ate neatly and quietly. He had served her first, filling her plate and passing it to her, and keeping her well supplied with wine.

"If your mother died when you were a bairn, who taught you your manners?" she asked without thinking. And then flushed. "I'm sorry. That was rude. I didn't mean—"

"No, it's all right. You can ask me anything." He quirked a brow at her. "My manners, is it? I trust you're not complaining about their lack."

Embarrassed, she shook her head. "On the contrary, they're very fine."

"I'm glad. Between my father, a very high stickler, you understand, Uncle Ian, more of a martinet than anything, and Uncle Charles, the quintessential courtier, I had no chance to be uncouth or unmannerly." He winked and added, "Uncouth I learned from Donald and Jimmy when they came to live with us." Jeannie had no trouble imagining that.

The pie was soon demolished, but somehow there was room for the rhubarb and apple pudding with dollops of thick, rich clotted cream on top. As they ate, Cameron entertained her with tales of the pranks he and his cousins got up to as lads. Until the arrival of the other boys, Cameron's life had been rather dull and duty-bound, she could see.

They finished eating, and Jeannie tidied away the plates, while Cameron refilled their wine glasses. He stirred up the fire and settled back. Clearly he was enjoying this relaxed talk as much as she was.

"You said you wore a sprig of white heather as a lad. Was that for one of the games you played with your cousins?"

"In a way." He grimaced. "It was a boyhood fancy—a sprig of white heather signifying the white cockade—the symbol of Bonnie Prince Charlie, a secret pledge to 'the king o'er the water'." He raised his own glass in an ironic salute.

"I grew up on my grandfathers' tales of the Bonnie Prince, you see, saw it all as a grand adventure, a romantic tale, dreaming of righting a great wrong, wishing I'd been born in their time. My father,

Uncle Ian and even Uncle Charles were the same. Dreaming of the glories of the past, and what might have—should have been." He gazed brooding into his wineglass. It glinted blood red in the firelight.

"Later, I realized the unpalatable truth." He drank deep of the wine.

"What truth was that?"

"That the bonnie prince, for all his charm and good intentions, and for all that he was entitled, he destroyed us, destroyed Scotland." There was a short silence, then he added, "Or, I don't know, maybe we destroyed ourselves."

He picked up some nuts and cracked them between his hands, picking out pieces of nut meat and passing them to her as he talked. "I visited Culloden Moor once, the place where it all finally came to naught, a nation to ruination. It's a dour, grim place. Haunted. The flower of Scottish manhood slaughtered, the very ground soaked with their blood. Leaving a generation of widows and orphaned bairns. And a nation divided, and given over to the ungentle mercy of the English."

Jeannie watched in silence as he sipped his wine, the strong column of his throat burnished bronze by the firelight, his eyes in some faraway time and place. She knew the tales, the bitterness and the vanquished dreams. It was all long in the past, but for many it was still a dream they kept alive. Looking backwards. *If only* . . . She'd heard it argued a thousand times.

"Now Scotland is left impoverished, and a new generation of braw Scots lads are off awa' to take the English king's shilling—German George's shilling—for the privilege of fighting in his wars across the sea. Because there's nothing for them at home. *Nothing!*" His fists bunched.

"And the Scots that aren't awa' fighting are leaving in droves; the lifeblood of the country, draining away overseas, to Canada, to America, and even as far as the Antipodes, on the other side of the world."

He tossed the nut shells into the fire and watched as they flamed and burned. "I want to build something *here*, at home, to make a future for my generation, men and the women both, and for their bairns—our bairns." He glanced at her. "Are you with me on this, lass?"

She nodded, swallowing the lump in her throat. This man, with his hard male beauty, strength tempered by honor, dreaming of a better future not only for himself, but for his people.

She told him then of her meeting with Uncle Charles and the women, and was gratified to see his eyes light up. He rose and held out his hand to help her up. "Aye, that's exactly what I'm talking about. 'Tis a grand idea, Jeannie. Those women are too proud to accept charity, but this way they keep their pride, and the extra money they earn will make for an easier winter for them and their bairns."

She nodded. "And their work will be on show for all who come here to admire, so it's not only fine ladies from Edinburgh who see it."

He drew her from her seat. "*And* it will keep Uncle Charles occupied and out of my hair, for which I cannot thank you enough."

He said nothing for a moment, just stood there holding her hand, and looking down at her. Then in a soft, deep voice he said, "T'was a blessed day, that day I pulled you from the bog, Jeannie McLeay Fraser. Are you a gift from the fairy folk, perhaps?"

She shook her head, feeling a little bashful under the warmth of his gaze. "Just an ordinary girl, I'm afraid."

"No' ordinary. No' the least bit ordinary. Not to me." He turned her hand over and, keeping his gaze locked with hers, he planted a slow kiss in the centre of her palm.

It shivered through her in a wave of warmth, and his words, well, they wrapped right around her heart. She gazed misty-eyed at the dark head bent over her hand. This dear, dear man. She loved him so much, it was fair bursting out of her.

Aye, she wanted him to love her, but you couldn't make someone love you. It happened or it didn't. And if he thought her extraordinary, and a gift, could that not be enough? Her father had been full of fine words and high-flying sentiments—he could fair break your heart with words, Da—but most men were not much for the words. It was actions with them, and she couldna fault Cameron's actions.

She thought of the way his hands had slipped over her skin in the bath, gentle and caressing and strong, melting her bones and turning her innards to honey. And he wanted her—that was clear—but he'd kept to his promise, turned his back to spare her blushes and stepped away, even though she could tell it half killed him. That promise was half killing her, as well.

What was she waiting for? The moment had come. Forget the poetry, the pretty words she'd yearned for, forget the fortnight she'd asked of him; she'd no' deny this darling man a minute longer.

She curled her hand around his jaw and raised his head. "Cameron, I know we've only known each other a short time, and you'll probably think it's foolish of me, and premature, but I think I'm falling in love with you."

She leaned forward and kissed him full on the mouth

Chapter Nineteen

SHE *LOVED* HIM? Cameron wanted to shout it from the battlements. His chest felt full and heavy. He struggled to find words to respond, but his heart was too full. He found himself saying gruffly, "It's neither foolish nor premature, Jeannie, but a proper thing in a bride." Sounding like an ancient graybeard, not a man whose heart was fit to bursting.

He knew she loved poetry, but there were no pretty words in him, just . . . *feelings*, too fierce and joyous and new to name. So all he could do was haul her into his arms and kiss her.

She slipped her hands under his shirt, over his chest, caressing his skin with small, work-roughened hands, finer to him than any lady's soft, pampered hands. And all the time kissing, kissing him hungrily, eagerly, as if she couldn't get enough of him.

He unfastened her dressing gown and slipped it off her shoulders. It slithered to the floor with a soft hush. Outside the rain was drumming on the roof and battering the window.

He felt her legs tremble and sag. His pulse leapt at this evidence of her arousal, but he reined himself in, and eased her over to the bed. He deepened the kiss, running his hands over her slender, lissome

body, caressing her through the soft, fine fabric of
her night rail.

She lay back on the bed, pulling him with her, and
he couldn't resist, though he knew he should, but
oh, she was so sweet, so eager and loving . . . He lay
on top of her, kissing, caressing, feeling the agony of
her softness positioned between his thighs, his bare
thighs—and bare everything else beneath the kilt.
The only barrier stopping them from joining was
the frail gossamer of her night-rail and the heavy
fabric of the kilt.

She pressed herself against him like a small eager
cat, writhing in innocent eroticism, her limbs
embracing him. She tasted of firelight and honey and
rain and salt and sweet, warm woman. His sweet,
warm woman, his Jeannie.

His kilt was riding up and as she moved she brushed
against him. Cameron groaned.He was hard and
throbbing and it was all he could do not to shove her
nightgown up and take her.

But he'd given her his word.

She brushed against him again. Dammit, he was
ready to spill. He pulled away abruptly and put
some space between them. He sat on the edge of the
bed, panting, trying to lash into obedience the wild
horses of his control.

"Cameron?" She touched him tentatively on the
shoulder.

He didn't reply. What the hell had happened? He
was as out of control as a young boy with his first
woman.

"Cameron?" She trailed her hand softly down his
spine.

He shuddered and arched beneath her touch.
"Don't do that!" There was a short, hurt silence

and he added in a quieter voice, "It's all right, lass. Just . . . don't touch me."

"Do you no' like me touching you?"

"I like it fine." Too fine.

"Then why?"

Och, the innocence of her. He closed his eyes a moment, then turned to explain. "Because it's stretching my control to its limits, that's why."

Her eyes dropped to where his sporran usually sat. "Your control?" There was almost a purr to the way she said it.

"Aye, touch me again and I'll be in danger of breaking my promise to you. And I don't break my word."

"I see." She tucked her legs beneath her, and knelt on the bed, watching him with those wide, considering blue eyes. It fair killed him the way she looked at him, and him not able to act on it.

The only sound in the room then was the crackling of the fire and Cameron's own heavy breathing. He tried to concentrate on pure thoughts, but the scent of her skin, of roses and warm, aroused woman teased his nostrils. Coals shifted in the fireplace and all he could think of was the way she would look clad in nothing but firelight. He gritted his teeth, willing his rampant body to obedience.

"What if I want you to?" The words came soft, wrapped in darkness.

His stomach lurched. Did she just say what he thought she'd said?

She leaned forward, her hands moved at his hips, there was the click of buckles and he felt his kilt begin to slide away. He grabbed it, clutching it against him. "What the hell?"

"I . . . I've changed my mind. I canna wait any

longer." She tugged gently at his kilt. "I want you now."

"But . . . I promised you a fortnight. It's only been eight days." And eight interminable nights.

Her eyes were luminous as she said, "I release you from your promise, husband."

He said nothing, just stared down at her, trying to breathe.

"The courtship is over, it's time to start the honeymoon." In one movement she pulled her nightgown over her head and knelt there, naked on the bed, her heart in her eyes.

His kilt fell away unnoticed as, with a groan, he pulled her to him. He lavished her with kisses, loving every inch of her skin with hands and mouth and body. She was warm satin, fragrant as petals and her hair flowed over her pale skin like the silky dark waters of a peaty burn.

She shuddered and gasped and pressed herself against him, wrapping her long silky legs around him, plastering him with hot, fervent kisses that drove him purely wild.

He'd planned to wait, to take it slow and gentle but she was wild and eager and impatient and so greedy for him he couldn't hold himself back.

"I love you, Cameron." There, she'd said it again, and again, his heart was fair to bursting.

He entered her with one long, slow thrust. He felt the barrier of her virginity, and checked as she gasped. But before he could say a word, her eyes met his. "Now, Cameron." And with a determined expression she lifted her body, thrusting against him, and he was in. And moving. And lost.

She cried out, arching and shuddering, clutching him with hard little fingers, her thighs trembling and closing around him as her body accepted him deep inside.Welcoming him.

Ancient rhythms pounded through him and at the spiraling edge of his awareness he heard a high, tremulous cry, and felt her shudder deeply as she shattered with him.

Cameron woke first in the morning. Usually he sprang out of bed, raring to meet the day. Now he lay quietly, listening to the soft sound of her breathing, examining the unaccustomed feelings that lay heavy and full in his chest.

This was how he'd wake every morning for the rest of his life. In bed with his wife, with Jeannie. Who loved him.

He felt . . . He tasted the feelings floating inside him. Happy. Humbled. Awed.

A little over a week ago he'd sworn a mad, rash vow and performed the most reckless act of a somewhat reckless life. It could have been the greatest mistake of his life.

He glanced at the girl curled up against him, her silky dark chestnut hair spilling over her shoulder, half hiding her face.

Instead she was the greatest gift.

He lay there, breathing her in, the scent of her; roses and woman. His woman, his bride. His . . . love.

The realization burst on him. Aye, she was his love. He loved her. Loved Jeannie. His Jeannie.

Her eyes fluttered open and she smiled sleepily. "Cameron," she breathed, and he couldn't help it, he had to kiss her, and then, well, he couldn't help himself again. He had no self-restraint, and apparently, neither had she.

Afterward they lay entwined, their breathing slowing, skin to skin, gazing into each other's eyes.

After a while she gave a shivery sigh. "That was the loveliest way to wake up." She stretched and gave him a rueful smile. "I suppose this means the courtship is over."

And she looked at him with that damned look in her eyes that shattered him every time.

He had to tell her. The feelings were like to burst out of him. But he had no words. And then he remembered . . .

Cameron took a deep breath and began.

"*My love is like a red, red rose*
That's sweetly sprung in June.
My love is like a melody
That's sweetly sung in tune—'" He broke off. She had tears in her eyes.

"What is it?" he said. "What's the matter?"

"Rabbie Burns," she whispered. "You're quoting Rabbie Burns to me." Great crystal tears glittered on her lashes. What the hell had he done wrong?

"You said you liked poetry."

"You said you didn't."

"Aye, well, I promised you a courtship. And you do smell like a rose, and so I thought . . ." He swallowed. "They fit. The words, I mean. They all fit. *All* the words." He scanned her face anxiously. Did she not see what he was trying to tell her?

He took a deep breath and broached the next verse.

"*So fair art thou, my bonnie lass,*
So deep in love am I,
And I will love thee still, my dear,
Till a' the seas gang dry.'"

Her mouth quivered. "In love, Cameron? Truly?"

"Deep in love."

"Is it Rabbie Burns speaking, or do you have words of your own?" She gave him that look and waited. Och, he was gone, he was truly gone.

"Perhaps one day I'll come to rue the day I plucked a wee bog sprite from the mud and married her, but I doubt it. Right now I think it's the cleverest thing I've done in all my life."

She tried to frown. "A bog sprite?"

Cameron grinned and kissed her. "Aye, a wee bog sprite who smells like a rose." He kissed her again. "My bonnie lass." And again. "My red, red rose." And then because she might not have understood what the poem meant, he cupped her face in his hands and, drowning in her blue, blue eyes, the words finally spilled out of him. "I love you, Jeannie McLeay Fraser, with all my heart. You're my blessing, and my gift, and my dearest, most beloved love. And och, you're no' in tears again, are you?"

"Happy tears," she wept, and he bent to kiss them away.

The End

THANK YOU FOR reading *The Laird's Bride*. I hope you enjoyed it.

Reviews help other readers find books. I appreciate all reviews whether long or short, positive or not.

Would you like to keep up with my news and be reminded when my next book becomes available? Sign up for my newsletter at:

www.annegracie.com

You can also sign up for my blog on the same page.

Follow me on BookBub:
https://www.bookbub.com/authors/anne-gracie

Follow me on twitter:
@AnneGracie

Like my Facebook Page: *http://facebook.com/annegracieauthor*

My Other Books

This is my second self-published novella.
If you'd like to read the first one,
The Christmas Bride, you can find it at:
https://books2read.com/u/3ydVap

THE BRIDES OF
BELLAIRE GARDENS series —
about the women who live and interact around the
beautiful Bellaire Gardens in London.

The Scoundrel's Daughter
The Rake's Daughter
The Heiress's Daughter
(coming May 2024)

THE CONVENIENT
MARRIAGE series —
about four women who in various ways get roped
into an unexpected marriage.
Marry in Haste
Marry in Scandal
Marry in Secret
Marry in Scarlet

THE CHANCE SISTERS series — about four sisters-of-the-heart, who take a risky chance to build a new life.

The Autumn Bride
The Winter Bride
The Christmas Bride (novella)
The Spring Bride
The Summer Bride

THE DEVIL RIDERS — about men who are back from the war and finding it difficult to adjust. The secret, they each learn, is finding the right woman.

The Stolen Princess
His Captive Lady
(also a readers' favorite hero)
To Catch a Bride
The Accidental Wedding
Bride By Mistake

THE 'PERFECT' SERIES — about the Merridew sisters who come to London to escape their horrid grandfather and seek their fortune.

The Perfect Rake
(still many readers' favorite hero)
The Perfect Waltz
The Perfect Stranger
The Perfect Kiss

I have also written two other Christmas novellas in anthologies with my fellow Word Wenches, and published by Kensington.

'*The Mistletoe Bride*' is in the anthology **Mischief and Mistletoe**

'*Mistletoe Kisses*" is in the anthology **The Last Chance Christmas Ball**

Thanks and Acknowledgements

THIS IS MY second venture into self publishing and the learning curve remains complicated, if also exciting. Thank you to the following writer friends for their help and encouragement: Alison Reynolds, Carol Marinelli, Fay Thomev, Merilyn Bourke, Pat Rice, Mary Jo Putney, Christina Courtenay and Kelly Hunter for feedback, advice and encouragement.

Thanks also to Kim Killion for my gorgeous new cover.

About Anne Gracie

ANNE GRACIE SPENT her childhood and youth on the move, thanks to her father's job which took them around the world. The roving life taught her that humor and love are universal languages and that favorite books can take you home, wherever you are.

Anne started her first novel while backpacking solo around the world, writing by hand in notebooks. Initially published by Harlequin, but mostly by Berkley (Penguin USA), her regency-era romances are national bestsellers in the USA, and have won many awards: the RWAustralia Romance of the Year (3 times), ARRA Favourite historical romance (9 times) and voted Australia's Favourite Author (5 times), among others. She also finalled in RWAmerica's RITA Award (5 times). Her books have been translated into more than eighteen languages and include Japanese manga editions (which she thinks is very cool). A lifelong advocate of universal literacy, Anne also writes books for adults just learning to read.

Made in United States
North Haven, CT
12 October 2023

42698289R00102